"I mean, there are some things that just aren't…well, negotiable."

"Really?" Ethan smiled. "Like what?"

"Well…toothpaste." Libby's parents were always arguing about that. "What if you like minty-fresh gel and I…I mean, your *spouse*, likes original flavor?"

"Two tubes." Ethan shrugged, and Libby wondered why her parents hadn't thought of that.

"There are, uh, other shared elements, you know." She blushed. "Like, well, married people generally share a…bed."

"We'll get a king-size if you like lots of room, a queen if you like to snuggle."

"I wasn't talking about the bed itself." She felt heat flood over her body as Ethan moved closer. "I was talking about…well, other things…other than snuggling. Or sleeping."

"Oh…" He raised his eyebrows. His voice dropped to a hushed, seductive whisper. "You meant…*sex*."

His hands moved to her shoulders, caressing her. Libby trembled, and her eyes drifted shut as he lowered his head.

"I don't think that's negotiable," he whispered. "We should definitely find out now if we're compatible…." And his lips met hers.

Dear Reader,

I don't know about you, but my family and I can't pass by a fountain without throwing a coin in and making a wish.

Gina, Libby and Jessie are just like me. When they find themselves at the world-famous Trevi Fountain, they send out their wishes for happiness on those gilt-edged coins they toss. But sometimes, no matter what we *say* we want, our hearts know what we *truly* need....

So it is for Libby here in Karen Toller Whittenburg's *If Wishes Were...Weddings* and for Jessie in Jo Leigh's *If Wishes Were...Daddies* (November), and how it was for Gina in last month's *If Wishes Were...Husbands* by Debbi Rawlins.

I'm happy to say that some of my wishes have come true.... Let's see how it works out for Gina, Libby and Jessie in THREE COINS IN A FOUNTAIN.

Happy reading!

Debra Matteucci
Senior Editor & Editorial Coordinator
Harlequin Books
300 East 42nd Street
New York, NY 10017

If Wishes Were...
WEDDINGS

KAREN TOLLER
WHITTENBURG

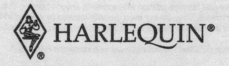

TORONTO • NEW YORK • LONDON
AMSTERDAM • PARIS • SYDNEY • HAMBURG
STOCKHOLM • ATHENS • TOKYO • MILAN • MADRID
PRAGUE • WARSAW • BUDAPEST • AUCKLAND

ISBN 0-373-16745-8

IF WISHES WERE…WEDDINGS

Copyright © 1998 by Karen Toller Whittenburg.

This edition published by arrangement with Harlequin Books S.A.

® and TM are trademarks of the publisher. Trademarks indicated with ® are registered in the United States Patent and Trademark Office, the Canadian Trade Marks Office and in other countries.

Printed in U.S.A.

Chapter One

Libby had never been in a man's bedroom before.

Except for her brothers' rooms. And her cousins'. And that one time at Billy John Burgess's house when he'd lured her into his bedroom and she'd had to kick him in both shins before he'd let her out. But this was different. There was romantic music playing. There was subdued lighting. Most important, there was a *man* in this bedroom...and he wasn't wearing any clothes. Well, at least the upper half of him wasn't wearing any, and Libby had a pretty strong suspicion that the part of him still under the covers wasn't, either. And she'd certainly never been in a *naked* man's bedroom before.

Of course, until yesterday, she'd never even been out of Texas.

"Libby?" He said her name with the same sultry Italian accent she'd found so mysterious and romantic back at the Austin airport, when he'd shown her preschool class their way around a jumbo jet. But here, in the Italian villa he'd described so vividly to her, she thought his accent sounded simply foreign. "Libby," he repeated, and rubbed his eyes, trying, she supposed, to wipe away the stunned dismay that was written all over his face. "Libby? What are you…?"

"Happy birthday," she offered, hope fading that he was going to remember he'd even told her today was his birthday, much less invited her to help him celebrate. "Do you want me to sing the birthday song to, uh, sort of wake you up?"

"No," he said decisively. "No, thank you. I'm awake. How did you…get here?"

"Airplane," she said briskly, wondering if she'd have come this far to see him if she'd known he had hair on his chest. She knew, of course, that men generally did have chest hair. But Nick had more than she was used to seeing, certainly more than her primarily bare-chested brothers. Not that she really minded, of course. It just sort of took her by surprise to see him without his clothes, that was all. She offered a brave little smile…and stayed close to the door as her voice rambled around in the red-faced silence. "My first experience with air travel. Maybe my last. Except, well, I'll have to fly home, of course, after the birthday party.''

This was embarrassing, she thought. Here she was, half a world away from home, face-to-face with the man she intended to marry. Well, at least, she'd intended to marry him until about two minutes ago when she'd caught her first glimpse of his chest hair. ''You know, it looks like you're pretty sleepy, so I'll just get on out of here and let you get your beauty rest.''

''I'm not so sleepy.'' He rubbed his eyes again, hard, as if hoping he could erase her from his line of vision. ''What are you doing here, Libby?''

Now, there was the sixty-four-thousand-dollar question, as Grampa George would say. Yesterday, when she'd boarded the transatlantic flight, she'd had the answer. Nick had said he'd be delighted if she could come to Rome for his birthday, so she'd impulsively decided to surprise him. And she'd surprised her family and friends with the news that she was going to Italy to marry the airline pilot who had stolen her heart with a kiss of her hand.

Okay, so in actuality, it had been the memory of his mouth-to-mouth kisses that had been the major factor in her decision. That and the fact that she'd just lost her job. And turned down Jason Joe Johnson's proposal of marriage. And needed to get out of town before her family and friends persuaded her to change her mind. So, all things considered, flying off to Italy on the spur of the moment had seemed like the perfect answer to everything. Perfect, at least, as long as Nick was still half a world away.

"I, uh, well, you did invite me to your birthday party," she said, feeling the blush rage in her cheeks. "And this is your birthday, isn't it?"

He glanced at his bare wrist, as if checking the time. "*Si.* Yes. My birthday. Of course." He tried to sound welcoming, a gracious host welcoming an anticipated guest. But the truth was, his voice didn't make the grade. The agitated way he ran his hands through his dark hair didn't do much to bolster his polite confirmation, either. Neither did his frown and doubtful "When did I...? Did you...? Did I *say* there would be a party?"

He hadn't meant it. She could see that now... along with his embarrassment and obvious consternation. It was becoming humiliatingly clear that she'd imagined the invitation, as well as the depth of his sincerity. How could she have fallen for his line?

On the other hand, how could she not have

fallen for him? He was, hands down, the most romantic man she'd met in all of her twenty-seven years. With one look, he had seemed to know all about her, what she longed for, what she needed. The problem, she realized now, was that there was a wealth of reality between a Texas wooing and an Italian bedroom. "You know, I don't believe you did say, specifically, that there would be a party. Guess I just assumed you'd be celebrating. Back home, birthdays are a pretty big deal, but probably you people do things differently." She couldn't believe she'd said that. "I mean, obviously, birthdays in Italy are different from the ones we have in Texas. Or maybe not. I mean, maybe you have cake and ice cream and presents and, uh, pony rides and pin the tail on the donkey games and...all that...party stuff." She edged toward the doorway. "Maybe it'd be better if I came back later in the day. Or later this week. Or just some other time. Sometime when you're not in bed. Sometime when you've got some, uh, clothes on."

"Buon compleano, Nicolo!" A woman swept into the room in a scented cloud of negligee, went immediately to the bed and gave Nick a resounding kiss. Her dark hair was disheveled, her gown beautifully seductive, and her voice rose and fell in a lilting barrage of Italian. At least, it lilted until she caught sight of Libby, at which point her dark eyes flashed and the foreign phrases picked up disbelief, accusation and a definite lack of welcome. Libby realized that the hours she'd spent with *Learn Italian in Ten Easy Lessons* were useless under the circumstances. And she had a feeling that asking the woman to speak slowly and distinctly wouldn't have helped much.

"Look," she said over the rapid-fire conversation bouncing between Nick, in bed, and the woman, in lavender. There was considerable passion ricocheting back and forth in their speech, and Libby felt decidedly uncomfortable eavesdropping, even though she couldn't understand one word of their argument. "You know, I think I'll just ease on out of here now and let the two of you work this out. If you could just point me in the general direction of the nearest hotel..."

The woman was pointing. Her lovely hands stirring the air with agitated gestures, her index finger leveled—now, and again—at Libby. As Grampa would say, you didn't have to be a weather vane to know which way the wind was blowing. Tucking her purse under her arm, Libby made a break for the doorway.

"Wait, Libby," Nick commanded, and she

stopped...mainly because the door was pushed open from outside and blocked her exit. A statuesque brunette stepped into the bedroom, her sultry voice preceding her by a breath. "Happy birthday, Nicky," she said.

"Gina?" Nick's hand rummaged through his hair again, as his gaze cut from the brunette in the doorway to the brunette in the negligee to Libby.

Libby stepped out from behind the door before it could open any wider and hit her square in the face. Someone gasped... Libby thought it was the brunette in lavender, but it could have been the tall brunette in the tight white T and the short, peach-colored skirt. In an instant, Libby assessed the Marilyn Monroe physique of the newcomer and the heaving bosoms of the Italian, and decided she was clearly outclassed by at least a cup size.

"Nick?" she questioned, wrapping her arms across her chest and reminding herself that there could be a perfectly logical explanation. These beautiful, busty women could be Nick's.... Libby couldn't think of a single relationship to explain the shocked looks on their faces. Well, technically, that wasn't true. She could think of *one*. Obviously, the party Nick had planned wasn't going to be anything like the birthday parties they had back home. "Nick," she murmured, in amazement and a stunned disbelief that she had flown all the way from Texas to be part of an...well, to be part of whatever the Italians called an orgy.

Into the awkward, music-filled moment, the curtains at the window fluttered, then flopped apart to admit a redhead, whose brilliant smile faded in increments of surprise, confusion, doubt and the bedroom standard—stunned disbelief.

Someone gasped. It could have been any one of the growing number of women who now stood in Dominic Carlucci's bedroom, but Libby thought it might have come from the depths of her own bruised vanity. "Nick," she said, sadly admitting what a fool she had been.

"Nick," said the brunette, the one Nick had called Gina.

"Nick," repeated the redhead.

The brunette in the negligee wasn't so succinct. She launched another round of outraged Italian, against which Nick didn't even attempt to defend himself. He just looked at them all in turn, the corners of his mouth lifting into a slightly sheepish grin. Then he said one word of Italian, with quiet authority, and the dark-eyed brunette abruptly shut up. He sat straighter in the bed and the covers slipped down, revealing that the wiry hair on his chest dipped lower than Libby had thought it would.

"What a surprise," he said. "How nice of you all to drop in."

"Drop in?" The tall brunette let the bag on her shoulder slide to the floor with a thud. "Drop *in?* I came all the way from Los Angeles. Three planes. No sleep. And I turned down two courier jobs. I did *not* just drop in."

Libby admired Gina's forthrightness and wished she, herself, had challenged Nick, instead of standing there, mute, while the man she'd intended to marry gathered his...his concubines. With a sudden, sobering insight, Libby remembered all the bridges she'd burned back in Beauregarde, just to get to this bedroom. "Oh, Nick," she said, her eyes widening at the memory. "I told *everyone* we were going to get married."

Libby felt the quick, cutting glance that Gina tossed her way and could all but read her thoughts. *You?* Gina might as well have said. *You thought he was going to* marry *you?* Libby couldn't stop her gaze from fleeing to the redhead, who was still standing in front of the window, looking rumpled but somehow serene and terribly dignified, despite the sprig of ivy sticking out of her hair. She didn't meet Libby's eyes, though, didn't, in fact, spare the other women in the room so much as another glance. She just stood there in her stocking feet, a runner as wide as the Blanco River stretching halfway up her calf, and focused all her energy on the man at the center of this bedroom farce. "So, it's like this, is it?" the woman asked, her arms crossed at her chest, like a sentry on duty. "It was all a game?"

"It was never a game," Nick answered quietly, his voice sounding dull and dismal against the background of an aria that soared and floated as romantically as a bird on the wing.

"You meant everything you said?" The red-head pressed him, never raising her voice, not even really accusing him, just stating the facts as she saw them. Libby turned back to Nick, startled to realize he probably *had* asked every woman in this room to marry him. Well, except he'd never actually asked *her*. He hadn't, as Jason Joe Johnson had at last Friday night's football game, said the words, *"Libby Ann Waldron, will you marry me?"* But she'd thought he meant to ask her. She really had. And she'd told everyone she meant to marry *him*.

Nick hesitated, ducked his head as his hand

made another pass through his tousled hair, then he glanced at Gina, Libby and the woman at the window. "Yes," he said.

"So you love all of us?"

"*Si*, Jessie, I love you all."

Libby tried not to let her mouth drop at that obvious fib, but she was aware of the beginning of a strange and welcome sensation...relief. "I can't believe I told everyone we were going to get married," she said, glad to hear a note of outrage in her words.

Turning her head, she looked at the three other women for support, bypassing the angry stare of the Italian *signorina* in favor of the warmer, sympathetic expressions of Gina and the redhead, Jessie, the one Nick's tones had caressed when he called her name. "What should we do now?" she asked them.

Jessie shook her head, but Gina gave an oh-the-hell-with-it shrug. "It is four to one," she said. "We could take him."

The idea held appeal, but one look at the dark-eyed brunette revealed a murderous gleam. Libby indicated the other woman with a nod. "I don't think she needs our help."

With a glance at Nick, Jessie sighed and squared her shoulders. "I saw a small bistro just down the road. I imagine they serve liquor there. It is Rome, after all. I think I'm about to get well and truly drunk.'' She offered Libby and Gina a ghost of a smile. ''If you'd care to join me?''

''Please stay, *cara mia*. I can explain everything.'' Nick sounded sincere, although Libby couldn't decide which one of them he was actually addressing. Then she realized he could be addressing all of them at once…a thought that oddly enough made her want to giggle.

''Count me in,'' Gina said to Jessie. ''I could use a shooter or two.''

''I'll go.'' Libby wasn't about to get left behind. ''I've never been drunk before, but this seems like the perfect time to get that way.''

''Yes,'' Jessie said, turning toward the door. ''It does, at that.''

Libby was the last of the three to pass through the doorway. She pulled the door closed, which somewhat muffled the sound of the lovely aria but didn't diminish the angry rattle of outraged Italian that erupted from behind the closed door. Nick was getting what he deserved on his birthday…and more. With a soft smile, Libby hurried after Gina and Jessie, glad she was no longer alone in Rome.

"TO TAR AND FEATHERS!"

Jessica lifted her wineglass and clinked it against Libby's, then Gina's. "Here, here."

"Ditto." Libby nodded before she took another enthusiastic drink of the wine, which tasted better with every sip. "Hot tar and boiling oil."

Gina grinned. "You guys are really getting the hang of this revenge scheme. I can't decide which one I like best. The honey and ants, a short walk out of a 747 at thirty thousand feet—"

"Without a parachute," Libby reminded her.

"Definitely without." Jessie swallowed the last of her wine and set her glass on the table, where it wobbled a second, then went still. "No parachute, tarred and feathered, ants all over him, at thirty thousand feet. I like it. The only thing that could make me happier would be if I got to *push* him out of the plane myself."

"Be my guest." Gina drained her wineglass and set it on the table next to Jessica's. "Personally, I think we're being too easy on the bastard."

Taking her cue from her new friends, Libby tipped the stem of her glass to the ceiling and swallowed the last drops of her new favorite beverage...cabernet. She could hardly believe she was sitting in a bistro in Rome, drinking wine with these two beautiful, sophisticated women. If

the people of Beauregarde could see her now...
On second thought, they were going to see her
soon enough as it was. That was a daunting
thought, recalling as it did her announcement to
a football stadium full of her friends and family
that she was refusing Jason Joe's proposal because she was in love with Nick Carlucci and was
flying to his villa in Rome to spend the rest of
her life with him. "Gina's right," she said firmly.
"Hot tar and boiling oil is too good for that two-
bit Lothario. We need to think of something really
bad."

"I've got it." Jessica smiled magnanimously.
"We can rent a billboard outside La Guardia airport and put up a wanted poster, warn other
women to watch out for the lying scum."

Gina looked at Jessie with sincere admiration.
"Great idea. I was leaning toward castration, but
the billboard is better. It's classy. Dignified, but
still down and dirty."

"I can't believe I spent so much money to
come here." Libby's train of thought jumped a
wine-soaked synapse from renting a billboard to
the state of her bank account. "I don't think I can
afford a billboard."

Jessica looked at her sympathetically and
sighed. "I spent a lot of money to get here, too.

It just goes to show that you can't trust them. Not ever. Men are louses." Her serene expression wrinkled with a frown. "Lice?"

"Jessie, girl, you've got that straight. Men are from Mars, all righty." Gina signaled the waiter for more wine. "The question is, how do we get them to go back?" She straightened and slapped the table. "Hey, a couple hundred torpedoes would do the trick."

Jessica giggled first, then Gina. Libby felt the effervescent sound bubbling out of her lips as well. It was a magnificent moment. Three women giggling...in a bistro...in Rome. Right after they'd found out their true love was a lying lice. Louse. Whatever. Libby was just happy to have something in common with Jessie and Gina. When the waiter came with more wine, Libby held out her glass, liking the wine, these two women and being drunk.

"I think..." Jessica leaned forward over the round wooden table and Libby leaned forward to listen. "I think we should make a pact. Right here. Right now."

Gina leaned in, too, and Jessica raised her head to look around the small bistro, making sure no one could eavesdrop. Libby checked, too, lifting her gaze to the waiter, the elderly woman behind the bar and the only other customer in the place...a man with his head stuck inside a newspaper. Of course, he could be a spy, pretending not to listen but actually recording their conversation for some sinister plot. Libby eyed the foreign headlines with a blurry frown and decided it took too much effort to read Italian.

"Well?" Gina asked. "Let's hear about this pact."

Jessie lost her faraway look and leaned into their friendly little circle again. "I say we swear off men for good."

Libby was ready to swear...right up until the last word. "For good?" she repeated doubtfully. "You mean, for the rest of our lives?"

"Yep," Jessie confirmed with a decisive nod.

"I don't know about that," Gina said. "They can be pretty useful on occasion."

"As far as I can tell, there's only one thing a man can do that's of any damn use at all."

"Yeah," Gina agreed. "But that one thing is a doozy."

Libby tried to follow their meaning, but there was a nice buzz inside her head and she decided it was just easier to ask. "What one thing?"

"We're New Age women," Jessie said. "And there are ways to get around that."

Libby wasn't sure a New Age woman would have flown all the way from Texas to find out she had imagined herself in love with a schmuck, but she wasn't going to say so. "Ways?" She mulled a sip of wine around her tongue before swallowing it. "What ways?"

Jessica and Gina both looked at her, then Jessica said, "Oh, come on, Libby. You've heard of Bob...our Battery-Operated Boyfriend?"

Libby giggled and hiccoughed at the same time. "Oh, sure, I've heard of him."

Gina stared at her for a second, then turned to Jessica. "Jessie, hon. I don't think the answer is to cut yourself off from men entirely. I think the trick is to know how to use them."

"Selectivity," Jessica said. "I can see your point."

"Right. Reel 'em in, throw back the little ones, put the big ones to work, then move on."

"Yeah," Jessica said. "Okay. Kind of like tissues. Take one, blow your nose, so to speak, then toss it."

"Sure," Gina said. "Why not? That way, there's no risk."

"Neat and tidy," Jessica added.

Libby frowned and turned her empty wineglass upside down on the table. She really didn't think disposable men were the answer. Maybe if they were more like handkerchiefs, which you could wash out and use several times before they got worn out. "Are you saying you never want to be in love, Jessie? Don't you want to get married and have kids?"

Jessica put down her glass, right side up. "Libby, honey, I don't want to tell you not to keep trying. That's totally up to you, and whatever you decide to do is great. But for me? I don't like the odds."

Gina reached across the table and wrapped one hand around Jessica's and one around Libby's. "Maybe you can beat the odds, Jessie. Maybe we all can."

"Maybe. But I'm not betting the farm on it."

Libby was beginning to feel a little melancholy herself. If Gina and Jessica were in her preschool class back home, she'd distract them with some cheerful activity, but what could she suggest here? *Here?* Was she kidding? They were in Rome, for Pete's sake! "Hey, you know what?"

Jessica looked at her. "What?"

Libby hiccoughed excitedly. "We're in Rome! And since we're here, I think we should go see the *fountain.*"

"What fountain?" Gina asked, taking one last sip of her wine.

"The Trevi Fountain," Libby answered. "Like in that movie, *Three Coins in the Fountain.* You know, these three women were in Rome and they threw a coin into the fountain and made a wish? And Rossano Brazzi was in it, too."

"Yeah, that's right. There was that French guy, too," Gina said, seeming to warm to the idea. "He was a count or something."

Libby turned to Jessica. "Didn't you see it?"

"Sure I did."

"Then what do you say?"

"Rossano Brazzi was a hunk," Jessica said with a slow smile as she got up from the table. "I imagine, for a handful of lira, we can arrange to leave our bags here and pick them up later. Do either one of you have any idea how to get to the Trevi Fountain or know enough Italian to ask directions?"

Gina stood, too, and pulled out her wallet. "I saw the fountain on my way to the villa. We can walk. It's not far."

"Great! Let's go." Libby opened her purse and the waiter appeared at her elbow as if he'd caught the scent of money. She didn't even bother trying to figure the lira into dollars. She just dumped a handful of coins into his palm and realized with a sinking heart that the money she'd exchanged at the airport was nearly gone. Rome was turning out to be one very expensive lesson. But at least she could say she'd seen the Trevi Fountain. Well, she could say that after she'd actually seen it and made her wish.

Outside, the afternoon sun wove a welcome mat of light and warm, fragrant air. Libby wondered if the sights and smells of Rome were as vivid and unforgettable as they seemed, or if the cabernet had merely sharpened her awareness and magnified the scene sprawled before her. Pedestrians, cars, bicycles and scooters raced like ribbons down the street while vendors and cafés lent color and texture to the sidewalks. *Rome.* Libby could hardly believe she was seeing it, and in her heart of hearts, she silently thanked Nick for inspiring her to come to this place of noise and nostalgia. Even if it was only for these few hours. Even if she couldn't stay long enough to really see the city. Even if she saw only one villa, one bistro, one famous fountain. But she'd be back. That was one reason she wanted to toss a coin into Trevi's fabled waters. She would make one wish, a wish to come back to Rome.

Libby saw it first, rising like a glistening mirage ahead of them. "There!" She pointed excitedly. "There it is! Wow! I had no idea it would be so big."

"Quite impressive, I have to admit," Jessie said.

"Excuse me, beautiful ladies." A boy approached them, his dark hair stringing across his dark eyes, his teeth flashing white with a cocky, winsome smile that held all the promise of fully developed Italian charm.

"Are you speaking to us?" Jessie asked.

"Beautiful lady, of course." The boy's voice hummed with persuasion beneath his heavily accented English. "You are the most pretty ladies here."

Gina frowned at the boy. "Shouldn't you be in school?"

The boy's smile brightened with determination and he put out his hand, palm up. "Five thousand lira, and I tell you about the Trevi Fountain. The legend, the history. Five thousand lira, beautiful ladies."

Libby was charmed, as much by the boy as by the idea of hearing all about the history and legend of this landmark. She was reaching into her purse and handed over the money. Gina added sternly, "You'd better not run off, kid."

"I am *Mario,*" he said as he stuffed the money into his pocket. Then, with a flash of a gap-toothed smile, Mario assumed his role as the keeper of legends. "This fountain, it is the most famous in all of Rome. There is a legend that if one throws a coin into the fountain, then one must return to Italy and to Rome and this place. But I will tell you another legend...one that only someone, such as myself, knows for truth. This legend, it is very powerful magic. When the coin first touches the water of Trevi, at that moment, if the heart makes a wish...it will come true. It cannot be otherwise. I tell you this because you are beautiful ladies and I wish for you that your special wish comes true."

"Is that right?" Jessica asked.

Mario didn't even blink beneath her doubtful frown. "I tell you, lady. For truth. You throw your coin in now. You make a wish. It come true."

Libby smiled, delighted with the boy and the fountain and the legend. She couldn't get a coin in her hand fast enough. It didn't matter to her that Gina looked openly skeptical or that Jessica seemed less than charmed by Mario's guarantees. Libby knew that in a few hours, she'd be on her way home. A few hours after that, she'd be face-to-face with the smug, we-told-you-so's and the sly glances and whispered asides of her family and friends, whose forgiveness would be harder to bear than their disapproval, who would now, piously, know for certain what was best for her. But for this moment, she was bathed in Italian sunlight and misted with water that flowed over sculptures she had only seen in books and movies. And, by gum, she was throwing in a coin and making a wish.

"Come on," she urged her new friends. "What have you got to lose?" Libby closed her eyes and concentrated on the weight of the small coin pressed tightly into her palm. She'd wish for nothing more than to return some day to this place, this city. Mum was the word to her foolish heart. It would probably wish for something dumb, anyway. Something like wishing she would fall in love with a man as romantic and passionate as Nick Carlucci...except not so foreign, not so promiscuous, and with less hair on his chest. Which would be a really dumb thing to wish for. Well, unless he was truly Mr. Right. Unless she could fall madly in love with him, and marry him before her family arrived at the airport to welcome her—and the husband they thought she was bringing—home. She flung the coin high into the air and watched it spin as it fell into the dark waters of the fountain.

Beside her, Gina made a pitcher's toss and her coin sailed through the air and landed near the statue.

"Your turn, Jessica," Libby said, wanting all three of them to be in on this adventure together.

Jessica shook her head. "I don't think so."

"Come on," Gina urged. "What's the worst that can happen?"

Jessica shook her head. But then she opened her purse and rummaged inside, finally pulling out a silver coin. She tossed it almost dispassionately into the fountain, where it landed with hardly a splash at all.

"Ah," Mario said from behind them. "Now, sorrowfully, beautiful ladies, I must tell you that only one wish will be granted."

"What?" Libby turned to face him, as did Gina and Jessica. "Why?"

"What kind of scam are you running, you little twerp?" Gina demanded.

Mario took a step back, at the same time giving a shrug of indefinable regret. "I only tell the legend, beautiful ladies. I don't make it up."

He melted into the crowd, leaving Libby feeling nearly as foolish as she had standing in Nick's villa while it filled up with heartbreak. With a smile that never quite made it to fruition, she looked at her companions…and in her foolish, selfish heart she wished, *Make it mine. Please, make it mine.*

Chapter Two

Ethan Redwine didn't need a canceled flight to ruin his day.

It had pretty much been shot to hell to begin with. As had been the past week, the current month and most of the year to date. Frustrated, he turned away from the Aria Italia reservations desk to check on his children, who sat huddled on their luggage like baby blue jays, grumpy and ungrateful.

There weren't many smiles in the whole airport—Italy took travel safety seriously—but there wasn't a pout anywhere as poignant or pragmatic as the one on the face of his eight-year-old son, Alex. And four-year-old Sallie wore the smudges of her endless tears with a world-weary dissatisfaction. And why shouldn't they be dissatisfied? Ethan thought. The world hadn't treated them to much of a childhood so far.

"When do we leave, Dad?" Alex demanded, even before Ethan knelt beside them. "How much longer do we have to stay here?"

"I don't wanna go." Sallie's straight black lashes were clumped and shiny, her round cheeks streaked with wetness, and her voice quivered with emotion as she lisped out a plaintive, "I wanna thtay with Neetha."

"Don't be such a crybaby." Unable to direct his own anger, Alex turned on his sister. "How many times do me and Dad have to tell you that Neesa's gonna marry Antonio? She's not comin' back home with us and she's not takin' care of you anymore."

Ethan shot his son a look. "Enough, already. Sallie understands. She just misses Neesa, that's all." He tried to gather his daughter into his arms, but she squirmed free of his comfort.

"I *don't* un'erthtand." Her tiny chin lifted defiantly. "I want Neetha!"

It struck Ethan that not once in the past fourteen hours had either of the children asked for Diane. Not that she'd been much of a mother to either one of them, but she was the best they had. Which was probably worse than having none at all. He'd been crazy to think this visit would change anything. "We'll find someone else to be your nanny," he said to Sallie. "And Neesa will write to you. She promised."

Sallie's lips trembled, and her voice stretched every vowel into an elongated whine. "I don't wan'er to write. I wan'er to be here now."

Ethan silently cursed all females old enough to fancy themselves in love and silly enough to think marriage was worth losing a good job for. He'd paid Neesa an astronomical salary to take care of his kids. Hell, he'd even paid her a sizable bonus plus expenses to accompany them to Rome, and look how she'd repaid him...by losing her heart to some slick Italian. Well, she wouldn't find another job as good as the one she'd had with him. Of that, Ethan was certain.

"When does our plane leave?" Alex asked, his impatient, disgruntled tone conveying a greater need for reassurance. "I'm ready to go."

Ethan gripped his son's shoulder and gave it a heartening squeeze. "There's been a delay, but the reservations clerk is trying to book us on another flight."

"How long is that gonna take?"

"Not long." He hoped.

"Daddy?" Sallie tugged on his pant leg. "I want to go."

"I know, sweetheart. I do, too." He patted her

head, wondering if he'd remembered to comb her straight, silky black hair before they left the hotel this morning, figuring it wouldn't have looked any different either way. "We'll be on the next flight to New York, I promise. Now, you two wait here where I can see you and don't talk to strangers and...well, just stay put. Understand?"

Without waiting for their replies, Ethan strode purposefully toward the counter, determined to beg, steal or bribe his way out of this country. The clerk, a young woman who had been something less than helpful up to this point, saw his approach and smiled. A good sign. Ethan picked up his pace, tripped suddenly and went sprawling across a tangle of legs and luggage.

His first reaction was annoyance that people couldn't keep their luggage and their legs out of his way. His first impression was of softness and shape and the faintly floral scent that was oh so familiar, and oh so elusive. Woman.

"Hey," she said, wiggling beneath him. "This airport obviously isn't big enough for the two of us. Would you mind getting off of me?"

She sounded so delightfully *not* foreign, it took him by surprise. American, for sure. And, if her accent was any clue, she hailed from somewhere far south of Fifth Avenue.

"Sheesh," she said, as she pulled herself out from under his weight and returned to a sitting position. "You Italian men are all alike. Step on a girl's heart, step on her ankle. It's all the same to you jerks. And not so much as a *scuzi* to soften the blow. You big lout."

Lout? Ethan rolled to his feet and stared at her, bemused, as she regrouped the scattered pieces of her belongings, all the while muttering to herself. She was slight but wore a voluminous dress that dusted her ankles and had no discernible fit to it. She wore boots, an amethyst pendant and a Mickey Mouse watch. Her hair was as thick and flyaway as Sallie's, but the color of corn silk and sunshine. Sections of it sprouted from her head in wild disarray, and there was a sooty smudge of mascara below each of her very blue eyes. Ethan opened his mouth to ask if she was all right.

"Signóre Redwine." His name flowed over the intercom in thickly accented Italian. "Signóre Ethan Redwine." Well, finally, he thought, glancing at the airline clerk, who motioned him toward the desk. Turning abruptly, he cast a hurried, *"Scuzi"* over his shoulder and headed for the reservations counter again.

"Daddy!" Sallie's voice trailed him, making sure he'd heard the summons. "Go, Daddy, go!"

He cast her a give-me-a-chance frown that hopefully would set her back on her suitcase until he could convince Aria Italia it was in everyone's best interest to fly the three of them out of Rome sooner rather than later.

LIBBY RUBBED HER ANKLE and decided, not for the first time, that she didn't much care for Italian men. First Nick broke her heart, and then this guy nearly broke her ankle. Not that she'd been in real danger on either count, but she was tired of getting stepped on. Staring at the man's broad back, she wondered how long she'd been asleep. The last thing she remembered was putting her head on her suitcase and wishing she knew what the person at the reservations desk had said to her about her return ticket. The next thing she knew, it was morning and she was being stepped on by an inconsiderate foreigner. Well, she supposed *she* was actually the foreigner here, but that didn't give him the right to step on her.

Feeling the weight of a serious gaze, Libby stopped massaging her ankle and looked up and into a pair of black eyes. The child was female, Eurasian and in obvious distress. Traces of tears spiked her lashes and shone in the depths of her beautiful eyes. "Hello," Libby said gently. "Where did you come from?"

"Go, pleathe." There was a tremor in the small voice, a hint of desperation, some lovely round vowels and a decided lisp.

Libby smiled. "You're American, aren't you? Either that or you speak better English than anyone else in this country. What's your name?"

The little girl blinked, her thick black lashes dusting her tear-smudged cheeks. "Thallie, go" she said.

"Thalliego." Libby rolled the name across her tongue. "Pleased to meet you, Thalliego. I'm Libby."

"I need to go."

"You need to go," Libby repeated. Then, with comprehension, she said, "Oh, your name is *Sallie* and you need to go to the bathroom."

Black hair swung forward as the child nodded vigorously in agreement.

Libby scanned the waiting area for a parent, someone who might match Sallie in features or in distress. But no one appeared to be missing one small girl. "Where's your mother?"

The child shifted from one foot to the other. "With Roberto, and *Ineedtogo.*"

Libby had seen that aggrieved look on the faces

of preschoolers before and knew that short of an announcement over the loudspeaker, there wasn't time to find Sallie's parents. And since an announcement would depend upon communicating with some airline clerk, it was clearly not an option. Gathering her bags, she managed to keep one hand free to clasp the little girl's fingers. "Well, Sallie, let's go find the bathroom, shall we?" Fully expecting Sallie's mother or someone called Roberto to appear at any second, Libby started toward the universal symbols that marked the public rest rooms.

But it wasn't a frantic parent who stopped her. It was a dour-faced man positioned right outside the bathroom door. The closer she got, the harder he scowled, and when she tried to pass him, he blocked her way. *"Fermi!"* he said roughly, shaking a jangly basket under her nose. *"Fermi!"*

She had never met such rude people in her life. Libby narrowed her eyes and lifted her eyebrows and once again tried to maneuver Sallie and the luggage past him and into the facility. No such luck. He stood his ground, reiterated whatever he was saying and rattled his basket some more.

Sallie squeezed Libby's fingers so hard, they nearly went numb. "Go," she whispered. "I need to go."

Libby turned back to the man. "Look, you, get out of my way. I'm taking this child to the bathroom, and if you try to stop me, I'm calling the police!"

"Polizia!" The man sounded indignant as he rattled the basket again. "One thousand lira or *polizia!"*

Sallie tugged on her hand. The man jangled the coins in his basket. Libby began to get the picture. "Lira?" she asked. "You want money?"

"Lira," he repeated. "One thousand lira."

Obviously, he expected to be paid a buzz-off fee before she was allowed to enter the bathroom. Now, what genius had come up with that idea? But it was pretty clear she wasn't going to get past him otherwise. Dropping her bags, Libby reached for her purse, but Sallie was clamped to her hand like a stick-tight burr. There was little choice but to swing the child into her arms and balance her weight against a hip while rooting out one thousand lira from the coins she'd been saving to take home as souvenirs. When she tossed them into his basket, the man nodded curtly and backed off.

With an indignant scowl of her own, she stepped around him and carried Sallie into the bathroom. From years of practice, Libby managed to help the child with her clothes and get her onto the toilet in record time, all the while keeping an eye on her own bags.

"Done." Sallie stood patiently while Libby kneeled down and readjusted her tights and corduroy jumper. Then she smiled, a bright, relieved, sunny smile, and threw her arms around Libby's neck. "I love you," she said.

Libby was used to being loved. Her preschoolers back home had been eternally eager to voice their emotions and distribute bone-crunching hugs. But somehow, in this noisy, foreign bathroom, her heart was touched by this small, solemn-eyed stranger, and Libby felt honored to be the recipient of Sallie's trust. She returned the hug, then straightened, returning Sallie to her hip in the process. "Let's get you back to your parents before they come looking for both of us, okay?"

Sallie nodded and looped her arms around Libby's neck. It took a minute, but Libby managed to regroup her bags and jostle them out the door. They'd barely stepped beyond the doorway and past the toll master when Sallie gasped. "I didn't flush!" she said, as if she'd committed some heinous crime. "Neetha thaid I alwayth havta fluth!"

"It's automatic," Libby began, but Sallie slid to the floor despite any effort to keep her from wriggling free. Like a shot, she raced back inside. With a hearty sigh, Libby went after her, bags and all...and was brought to an ignominious halt by the man with the basket. "Lira," he said firmly. "One thousand lira."

"No, you don't understand. I don't want to use the facilities," Libby explained with carefully contained impatience. "I just need to keep an eye on that little girl."

He rattled the basket again. "Lira. One thousand lira."

Furious with the man, the airport and the whole country, Libby dug into her purse and pulled out another handful of coins, not caring if she gave him five hundred lira or five thousand. At this rate, the next time she passed through these portals, she'd have to take out a loan just to pay for the dubious honor of flushing an Italian toilet. "There, you greedy little man," she said as she tossed the coins into his waiting basket. "Count that."

"*Grazie!*" he said, and when he turned to rattle the basket at some other unsuspecting tourist, Libby shoved her bags through the doorway and went in after Sallie.

"WHAT DO YOU MEAN, you don't know where she went?" Ethan shoved a hand through his dark hair and scanned the waiting area for a sign of his daughter. "I thought I told you to keep an eye on her."

Alex shrugged and kept his nose buried in the handheld video game he was never without. "She said she had to go to the bathroom," he said, as if that excused him of any responsibility.

"So why didn't you take her?"

Alex looked up, just long enough to display his disgust at that idea. "You said to stay put and I did. Sallie's the one you should be mad at, not me."

"I'm not mad at either one of you," Ethan said, although that wasn't entirely true. He was mad at everyone. "But you shouldn't have let her go off by herself."

"She's not by herself." Alex manipulated the control buttons with methodical precision. "That lady's with her."

"What lady?"

"That one you tripped over. The one with the weird hair."

Panic bloomed, complete with visions of Sallie's hair sprouting up all over her head. "Sallie barely even talks to you and me. She wouldn't go off somewhere with a stranger.''

Alex frowned and kept playing. Obviously, brotherly concern stopped at the boundaries of Game Boy. ''Well, where'd they go?'' Ethan demanded. ''Did you at least see where the woman went with Sallie?''

Alex took his time answering. ''Bathroom, I guess.''

''Bathroom,'' Ethan repeated, searching for the signs. ''I turn my back for five minutes and some wiggy woman kidnaps my daughter.''

Kidnap. The word sounded harsh and ridiculous and scary. Very scary. ''You stay here,'' he said to Alex, and wished he had someone, anyone, to help him watch out for the two kids he'd moved heaven and earth to call his. ''I mean it, Alex. I want to find you right here when I get back. Got it?''

''Got it.'' He answered without once glancing up from the video game.

Tired, irritable and now worried, Ethan kept Alex in view as he made his way through a sudden influx of passengers in the waiting area. He scanned the crowd, then looked back to check on his son, then searched again for a glimpse of Sallie's blue jumper and blue-black hair. She was okay, she was safe, he told himself. Any second he'd see her, wandering around. The blonde who'd tripped him had been American. Sallie might have seen her as more familiar. But he couldn't see his daughter taking up with a stranger, no matter her nationality. And how could he even be sure the blond woman was the one who'd taken Sallie? For all he knew, his daughter could have decided to tackle the bathroom on her own. Not likely, though. Not likely at all.

"I *told* you, I don't want to use your darn old bathroom. I just want to go in and get the luggage I had to leave in there when this child ran out ahead of me. Now, step aside, you big, hairy lout!"

Lout? What were the odds of there being two people in the Leonardo da Vinci airport who would use that word? Ethan skirted a family of five and caught a glimpse of his quarry...sprouts of blond. Pushing past a man in a business suit, he saw the woman conversing loudly with the rest room attendant, who was conversing back in rapid-fire Italian and wild gestures. Ethan's knees went weak at the sight of Sallie, nestled on the blonde's hip like a koala cub clinging to its mother.

"Sallie!" he said with loud relief, and reached for his daughter, jerking her unceremoniously into his arms and hugging her tightly. "I was so worried. You should never have wandered away like that." He glared accusingly at the woman. "What the hell were you doing with my daughter?"

Blue eyes met his with disbelief. "Well, what do you *think* I was doing? She asked me to take her to the bathroom and I did...at some expense, I might add."

"Is that true, Sallie? Did you ask this woman to take you to the bathroom?"

Sallie nodded and reached her arms out to the blonde, as if Ethan were the stranger. He shifted her firmly to one side.

"She doesn't usually talk to strangers," he began, as a segue into a somewhat sheepish thank-you. "She usually doesn't talk much at all...to anyone."

"I think she was a little desperate," the woman said, and took a step toward the bathroom.

The attendant vigorously jangled the coins in his basket. "Lira," he repeated. "One thousand lira."

She frowned at the attendant, then jerked her thumb at Ethan. "He'll pay," she said. "I'm going in to get my bags." And with that, she marched into the bathroom.

"Libby!" Sallie cried out as if she were losing her best friend, and wiggled in Ethan's arms. "I want Libby!"

The attendant rattled off a threat and shook the basket. "Lira," he said. "One thousand lira!"

Ethan looked from his daughter to the attendant to the basket being waved under his nose. On top of everything else, it looked as if he was going to have to pay one thousand lira to apologize.

WHEN LIBBY CAME OUT, Sallie was on the ground and attacked her with knee-crunching enthusiasm. "Libby! Libby!" Sallie said. "You came back!"

Libby dropped her luggage and sidled away from the doorway with forty pounds of little girl attached to her knees. "I had to get my suitcase before someone took off with it," she explained to the child, but her eyes were on Sallie's father. A tall man, he was darkly handsome, and Libby decided that anyone he stepped on might easily have mistaken him for an Italian. Except for the sheepish look in his eyes.

"She really likes you," he offered as an opener.

"I have that effect on kids and puppies." Libby

tried to loosen Sallie's stranglehold to no avail. "Sometimes I think the words *I teach preschool* are written across my forehead."

"Sallie couldn't read them, even if they were." He leaned down and grasped Sallie's arms, which consequently tightened around Libby's knees. "Come on, Sallie. Let go of the nice lady."

"No."

Libby met his gaze and offered a little smile of encouragement.

"Sallie, I need you to take hold of my hand so we can go back and see what Alex is doing. He must be wondering where you are right about now."

"No."

"Sallie." His tone turned into a warning. "Let go."

"No."

Libby was a bit surprised by the strength of Sallie's protest. She'd played out this scene before with other children, but usually there was only a moment or two of resistance before the child yielded to the parent's wishes. But Sallie didn't show any sign of letting go...and Libby certainly wasn't going anywhere. Any movement was bound to topple both her and Sallie.

"Sallie..." His drawn-out threat was clear, but

the child simply buried her face in the folds of Libby's dress. Almost without thinking, Libby dropped her hand onto the little girl's head.

Sallie's father looked from the hand to Libby's face, then he straightened and offered an apologetic smile. "Since my daughter seems to have temporarily cemented herself to your legs, perhaps I should introduce myself." He extended a large hand. "Ethan Redwine."

Libby dropped her hand into his...and her fingers were very nearly swallowed up in his palm. "Libby Waldron," she said. "I'm pleased to meet you. You have a charming daughter."

"A little less than charming at the moment, but she's exhausted." He cast a sympathetic glance at Sallie's bent head. "It's been a disappointing...vacation for her."

His smile was weary, and it changed her impression of him in an instant. Suddenly, she saw him not just as a harried father in an airport, but as a man who'd been disillusioned and disappointed, but who was not and would not be defeated. Libby wondered how she could have mistaken him for anything other than American. Sure, he had the dark good looks of so many Italian men, but in her brief experience, men of the U.S.A. had a certain confidence, an ease of manner, a deep sense of self they carried with them. And Ethan Redwine had it in spades. "I'm sorry Sallie bothered you," he said. "I'll be happy to refund any lira you had to spend on her behalf."

"Thanks for offering, but, to tell the truth, I'm not sure I want to take home anything from this place. Italy has lost some of its charm for me in the last twenty-four hours."

"Did your flight get canceled, too?"

She glanced at the lineup at the reservations desk. "I don't think I had a flight. I talked to the reservations clerk when I got here last night, but to be honest, I didn't understand anything he said. And then I fell asleep and..."

"You've been in the airport since last night?"

Libby frowned, wondering why her memory was so vague on details. "Have you ever had cabernet?"

There was a slight tug of humor at the corners of his mouth. "I have. On occasion."

"Well, I hadn't. Until yesterday—and don't get me wrong, I really liked it—but it made me sort of sleepy, and I can't exactly remember everything that happened. Well, except for the fact that I spent way too much money getting here, and now I've got no choice but to go home." The idea of going home was disturbing. It was true that there was no place like home. But not when going home involved some real, tall explaining to do once she got there. Sallie tugged on her skirt.

Libby leaned down.

"Libby?" she whispered.

"Yes, Sallie?"

"Go, pleathe."

"You need to go to the bathroom, again?"

Sallie shook her head. "Home."

"Home," Libby repeated. "You want to go home."

Sallie nodded and began to cry. Ethan bent swiftly and lifted her into his arms. "We *are* going home, pumpkin. I've got our tickets in my pocket right now. We'll be home before you know it, I promise." He looked at Libby. "She's not usually this unhappy. It's been a bad week."

"Must be an epidemic." Libby grabbed the straps of her luggage and swung first one bag, then the other, onto either shoulder. "Guess I'd better see about getting my ticket changed, because I certainly don't want to spend another night in this place."

"Airports don't make great hotels."

"The airport isn't so bad. It's the country I object to."

"Well," Ethan said. "Thanks again. And good

luck on getting your ticket changed. If I were you, I'd be prepared to upgrade. They've canceled all but a couple of flights to the U.S. today, and the only seats left are first class.''

Libby sagged against the wall behind her. ''Well, guess that means I'll be spending more time in this airport. There's no way I can afford to pay for first class.''

''Maybe you'll get lucky and be upgraded for free.''

She glanced at the reservations desk again—the long lineup wasn't promising. ''Thanks. Looks like I'll need to get very lucky.''

Ethan started to say something, she could tell. But he didn't. He just patted Sallie's back and turned to leave.

''Libby!'' Sallie shrieked. ''Libby, go! I want Libby!''

Abruptly, Ethan turned back . ''If I can get you a ticket, would you consider sitting with Sallie on the plane?''

''What?''

''I'll pay you two hundred dollars and cover the cost of your ticket.''

Libby blinked, surprised as much by the offer as by the note of desperation in his voice. Ethan

Redwine didn't seem like a man who would be desperate...for any reason. "Well, I—"

"Look. I know that probably sounded a little crazy, but it would make the long trip easier for Sallie. As I said before, it's been a really bad week for her."

Sallie's sniffles confirmed it, and Libby's heart went out to both daughter and father. "Well, it would be nice to have company," she said tentatively. "And a ticket on the first plane out of here."

"Great," Ethan said. "Perfect. I'll see about getting you a seat on our flight." He turned away, then turned back. "Did you check any luggage?"

"What you see here is all the baggage I have."

"Great," he said. "Perfect."

Libby smiled. "Here, why don't I watch Sallie while you get things taken care of?"

"Great," Ethan said as he handed over his daughter, who nestled against Libby's shoulder as if she'd always done so. "Perfect." He started to leave, then turned back. "Uh, would you mind watching her over there?" He pointed to where a dark-haired boy sat on a layer of suitcases. "And could you maybe keep an eye on my son, Alex, too?"

Libby nodded, wondering what she'd just

signed up for and where these two children's mother was and why this had been such a bad week. But what she said was "Sure, I'm happy to help."

He turned away, striding confidently toward the reservations desk.

"Uh, Mr. Redwine? Ethan?" Libby called after him, realizing suddenly the question she should have asked first. "Where am I getting a ticket to?"

But he didn't hear her. Libby shifted Sallie's weight onto her hip and asked, "Well, Sallie, where's home? Los Angeles? New York? Timbuktu?"

Sallie nodded in answer to each suggestion and hugged Libby ferociously. "Libby, home," she said.

Some things had a way of working out, Libby decided. Because no matter what her new destination turned out to be, no matter where Ethan Redwine hung his hat, it wouldn't be Beauregarde, Texas.

Chapter Three

"Then we pull back the ends like this, and presto, there are two little babies sleeping in a cradle, see?" Libby demonstrated how to rock the handkerchief cradle, then offered it to Sallie, who took it with such enthusiasm that the folds of the material collapsed and the pretense was lost.

"Uh-oh," Libby said. "Want me to show you how to do it?"

Sallie nodded eagerly, and Libby smoothed the handkerchief on her lap. "First you fold it into a square, see? Now, roll that end into the center. That's good, Sallie. Then you do the same with this end. Right. Now, here's the tricky part. Hold this together with that hand and pull on this with your other hand and there you go...two little babies in a cradle."

Sallie smiled broadly, the way she had the first

time she wrote her name, and rocked the handkerchief, carefully this time and with innocent
pride. Watching from across the aisle, Ethan
couldn't believe how well this was turning out.
Sallie hadn't cried a single tear since getting into
her airline seat next to Libby. She'd talked more
than she had in weeks, too, wiping away at least
some of his concern that she'd forgotten how.
Ethan congratulated himself. Sometimes he had
really good ideas, but once in a while, he had
genuine flashes of brilliance. And getting Libby a
ticket in exchange for her help with the kids had
been a stroke of genius. Opening his briefcase, he
pulled out the file on the Merritt Hotel chain and
went to work.

ALEX LEANED ACROSS the aisle, mesmerized by
the video game in Libby's hands. Her thumbs manipulated the controls with blinding precision...or
at least, enough speed to impress one eight-year-
old boy. Little blips sounded in tiny cheers with
every point won, and from the sound of it, Libby
was racking up quite a score. Ethan leaned forward, pretending a need to get closer to the paperwork in front of him, but in reality, he simply
wanted a better view of Libby. One not blocked
by the up-and-down movements of Alex's dark

head. Ethan had spent a good portion of the two hours they'd been in the air watching Libby. He told himself he was merely interested in how she'd managed to capture his children's trust with such apparent ease, but as time passed, he admitted that Libby was extraordinarily easy on the eyes. Any man would have taken the opportunity to admire her. At some point, she'd combed her hair and tamed the sprouts. And wiped the smudges from her cheeks. And—although he wasn't entirely sure about this—it looked as if she'd powdered the shine off her nose.

He was rather smitten with her nose and the cute little upturn at the tip, which was quite fetching. Every time she looked at him, he was surprised at how beautifully blue her eyes appeared and how very dark and thick her lashes were. All in all, Libby was a find, a bonus in a week woefully short on lucky breaks. She was pretty and she was good with kids. Great with kids, actually. He'd never have been able to keep Alex and Sallie so entertained. They'd have been lucky to make it home without one or all three of them seceding from the family union. There'd have been more pouting, more tears, more trauma…if they hadn't met Libby.

Ethan toyed with the possibility of asking her

to take Neesa's place as nanny. He'd want to talk to her, find out a bit more about her, maybe check her references, too, but if Sallie, who normally didn't put any faith in strangers, had decided that Libby was okay...well, Ethan wasn't going to question that small gift of trust.

Convincing Libby to take the position might prove to be the main obstacle, but Ethan was in the business of convincing people, and he had no doubt he could offer enough incentive to lure Libby from her current job. Preschool teacher, he thought with a sort of gleeful satisfaction. This was just nearly perfect.

"Wow!" Alex said in a voice of awed respect. "How'd you learn to do that?"

Libby laughed and handed the game back. "I have seven nephews who are constantly challenging me to video game duels. I either had to learn to play or find some other way to impress them."

Ethan liked her laugh. He liked the soft Texas drawl in her voice. He could interview a dozen candidates to be Alex and Sallie's new nanny and not find anyone half so delightful as Libby. She liked kids. More to the point, she liked *his* kids. They liked her. He liked her. It was a match made in heaven, as far as Ethan could see. He decided he'd persuade her to take the position just until he'd concluded the Merritt Hotel contract dispute. He'd couch the offer to Libby in terms that would appeal to a Good Samaritan, probably something along the lines of ''would she help him with the kids until he could find the right person to take Neesa's place.'' Then, he'd do all he could to convince her to stay permanently.

One of the first rules of negotiating was to appear enthusiastic, but not overly eager. He didn't want Libby to know what a help it would be to him if she took the position. Why wouldn't she accept the job, though? He was a good employer and he could afford to be flexible. But he had to be careful. Sallie and Alex had had one too many goodbyes already, and Ethan intended to do everything possible to ensure that the next caregiver in their lives would stick around for a long while. He'd lost the last employee he intended to lose to foolish romantic nonsense. And he was writing *that* into the contract.

SALLIE WAS SPRAWLING in her sleep, edging slowly but surely onto Libby's lap. Ethan took advantage of the opportunity to shift a yawning Alex into the vacant seat in the next row and suggested that Libby sit in Alex's now vacant seat next to him.

"I don't mind holding her," Libby said. "She isn't heavy."

"But she is restless. You'll be more comfortable over here and so will she." Ethan shuffled papers and then began putting them away, as if that were an incentive. "Besides, it'll be easier to talk to you if you're not sitting across the aisle."

Libby looked startled, as if the idea that he wanted to talk to her was strange and warranted caution. But she unfastened her seat belt and moved over into the seat beside him. He was instantly aware of the warm, pleasurable feeling that came from being near a pretty girl. Woman, he corrected himself. For all her youthful appearance, Libby was definitely a woman, with all the prerequisite and seductive angles.

"I thought you needed to work." She snapped the buckle of her seat belt and gave him a smile that turned the warm, pleasurable feeling into something more. "I thought that's why you bought my ticket. So I could watch the kids and you would have the travel time to work."

"All work and no play..." he said with a shrug.

"Or all ants and no picnic, as my grampa George would say. Or all lumber and no toothpicks, as my uncle Twig would put it. Or all garden and no party, according to my aunt Azalea.''

"Uncle Twig? Aunt Azalea?'' He smiled. "You're putting me on.''

"No, really. My family has a thing about nicknames. I gave up trying to explain them years ago.''

"So there's a reason your uncle is called Twig?''

"He runs a lumberyard, and Aunt Azalea is our town florist, but most of the nicknames aren't that logical. Uncle Shake, for one. Uncle Knot, for another. And if you can figure out why my aunt Marilee is called Pip, I'd be very grateful if you could explain it to me.''

"Mmm. Maybe she's a pip-squeak.''

"I already thought of that. Truth to tell, I don't believe anyone remembers how she came by such a nickname.''

"So what's yours?''

"My theory on Aunt Pip?''

"No, your nickname.''

"I'm not going to tell you that,'' she said firmly. "Not even if the plane were about to crash and I knew absolutely you'd never tell another living soul.''

His curiosity was aroused. "Now, that's intriguing. If I find out, can I call you by this family nickname?"

"Not if you want me to answer."

"Do you ignore your whole family when they do it?"

"Ignoring all of them would be impossible."

"Big family?"

"*Big* family," she confirmed, her lips curving with wry affection. "Even for Texas, where everything is bigger. At the last christening, there were fifty-seven of us Waldrons. And that's not counting the distant cousins, the ones who don't live in Beauregarde."

Beauregarde, Texas. Ethan made a mental note. "I'm an only child," he said. "There are some cousins on my mother's side, but I probably haven't seen them more than five times in my life."

"I can't imagine what that must be like. Seems as if I've been surrounded by aunts and uncles and cousins since day one." She paused, then smiled. "Comes of growing up in a small town, I guess. Even people who aren't blood kin think they're your family and that it's their duty to tell you what to do. Where did you grow up?"

"Detroit."

"Detroit," she repeated. "Oh."

Ethan grinned. "Don't sound so unimpressed. Detroit may not be in Texas, but it's sizable just the same."

"I'm really not one of those obnoxious 'the rest of the country is just a suburb of Texas' people. It's just that when you've never been anywhere else, you tend to buy into the idea that the rest of the world could fit inside the state borders…with room to spare."

Ethan watched her adjust the seat back, then the seat belt. "But you have been out of Texas. You've been to Europe."

She looked at him, clearly surprised by the thought, and then laughed softly. "I have, haven't I. I've been to Italy."

"I take it this was your first trip abroad?"

"First trip out of Texas. I was beginning to think I'd never see a city bigger than Dallas or Houston, and now I've been to Rome. Wow."

"That ought to impress the kinfolk back home in…Beauregarde, did you say?"

"Beauregarde," she confirmed, clasping her hands and then, just as quickly, unclasping them. "And the people there aren't that easy to impress. Especially as I only spent one night in Italy, barely enough to say I was there. But I did get to toss a coin into the Trevi Fountain and make a wish. Not that I'm in any hurry to return to Rome, you understand—which is what I was told the wish is supposed to be—but someday I might want to go back."

"I'd be happy never to see that country again."

"Why?"

He frowned, not wanting to get into the whole sordid tale of Diane and Roberto. "Let's just say I didn't find Italy as charming as the travel brochures promise."

"I have to admit Italy didn't turn out to be as…well, as romantic as I'd been led to believe, either."

"Romantic?" The word alone gave him pause. "Ah, now, you're going to spoil my initial impression of you, Libby. Here I've been thinking you're a very intelligent, very independent American woman who would never fall for some slick Italian charmer, and you start sounding like you've left your one true love at the Trevi Fountain."

"I left him in his villa," she said crisply. "In bed with a busty brunette."

Ethan's eyebrows rose in spontaneous surprise. "You're kidding," he said.

"Believe me, it wasn't very funny."

"The man must be a complete idiot."

Warm color flooded her cheeks. "*I* was the idiot to fly halfway around the world for him. And he turned out to be so…so *lousy*. But you know what? That's one mistake I will never make again. In fact, I don't want to waste another second talking about him, so just forget I mentioned that embarrassing event, would you, please?"

"It's forgotten." He found it difficult to believe any man would have tossed Libby over for a sultry brunette…she would have had to be sultry, he decided, to top Libby's delightfully genuine innocence. But no matter what had actually happened back in Rome, her broken heart worked to his advantage. "So, how many broken hearts did you leave back in Texas?"

"Let's not talk about that, either."

"That many, huh?" He smiled, encouraging trust. "See, my image of you was right. You're too bright and savvy to fall for a bunch of romantic nonsense, whether it's served up Italian or Texas-style."

She fidgeted with the folds of her dress, an action Ethan noticed, and noted, with interest. "I am," she said suddenly, as if the idea became steadily more appealing to her. "Romantic nonsense is just nonsense, and I'm too smart to fall for it ever again. That's why I've sworn off men for good."

He almost laughed aloud at that, but a disgruntled woman who'd been betrayed by her lover was perfect for what Ethan had in mind. Just perfect. "Smartest thing you could do," he said. "I've made a similar vow about women."

Her eyes were wide and so incredibly blue a man could get lost in them. A man who was susceptible to that sort of thing, of course. "Really?" she asked. "What happened to you?"

"My ex-wife," Ethan said, and changed the subject. "Did you say you teach preschool?"

"Yes." Her whole expression brightened, as if she couldn't believe he'd remembered that about her. Then, just as suddenly, her bright expression dimmed. "At least, I did. Well, I'm still a teacher, just an unemployed one at the moment. The child care center where I worked closed its doors a couple of weeks ago. That's one of the reasons I went to Rome."

"Oh?" Ethan made it a question, even though he really didn't care why she'd gone to Italy as long as she didn't want to go back. "Were you looking for a job overseas?"

"No." She sounded definite about that. "I told myself it would be a little vacation before I had to start searching for another position, but it didn't work out quite the way I'd envisioned it. For one thing, it was a lot more expensive than I thought it'd be and for another...well, we're not going to talk about that.''

"The idiot," Ethan said. "I remember. No, scratch that. I've forgotten all about him.''

"Yes, me, too," she agreed. "I'll need to start sending out résumés as soon as I get home. Maybe I'll send some to Detroit.''

"Why don't you send some to New York? That's where I live now.''

Her blush returned, even though it hadn't entirely ebbed away from before. "Oh, gee, I didn't mean to sound like...I wasn't trying to...well, you just mentioned Detroit and that's why it popped into my head. It wasn't because I thought you lived there. Uh, would you mind just forgetting I said that, too?''

"At the rate you're asking me to forget things, it's going to be hard to get to know you, Libby. Let's see, if I've forgotten about the idiot in Rome and where you're going to send résumés, and we're not going to talk about the broken hearts back home, then we'd better jump back to the 'never been anywhere except Rome and Texas' topic." He loved the way she pursed her lips at his teasing, found the little dimple near the corner of her mouth enchanting. "So," he continued, "I guess it's safe to assume that since New York City isn't in Texas, you've never been there, either?"

The dimple vanished as she shook her head no. "Small-town girls are encouraged to think of the Big Apple as rotten through and through."

"Oh, but it isn't like that at all." He settled back and began to lay the subtle groundwork of persuasion. "There are some rotten things, sure, but mostly it's a great place to live and work. And you can't tell me Houston and Dallas don't have their seamy sides."

"We're not encouraged to explore those cities, either. Certainly not without *appropriate* male protection. Small towns generally are equal opportunity when it comes to closed minds. You get the idea...if it doesn't happen in Beauregarde, then it's most likely contributing to the overall decay of our society and shouldn't be happening anywhere else, either."

"The residents are big on rot and decay, huh?"

"Just on keeping it out of our fair city."

"So does everyone get inoculated before they leave town?"

"We all have to be decontaminated before

we're let back in," she said with a smile. "It's really not that bad, though. I exaggerate because I've never been away long enough to know what kind of 'rot and decay' are even out there."

"Didn't you go away to college?"

"My dad got sick my senior year in high school and I had to stick close to home to help run the family hardware store. So instead of going away to school, I drove back and forth to Southwest Texas State in a car handed down through my three older brothers. By my junior year, Dad was okay, but by then it was too late for the dormitory experience, so I just kept on commuting. If I'd ever calculated the mileage, I'm sure a round trip to every state in the union wouldn't have burned up the same amount of miles I covered going between Beauregarde and San Marcos."

"No wonder you jumped ship and flew off to Rome when your job fizzled out."

"Yeah, no wonder." She looked down at her hands, then up at him. "What were you doing in Rome?"

"Retrieving my kids," he said. "Say…why don't you spend a few days in New York City? There's really no reason not to give the place a chance, if only so you can report back to the folks at home that it isn't quite as rotten as they imagined.''

''I wish I could.''

''What's stopping you? You said you didn't have a job to go back to, and as far as I can tell, you're over twenty-one and free to do what you want.''

''Yes, well, there's a catch-22 in freedom, you know. Not having a job means not having a paycheck, and *not* spending a few days in the Big Apple, even though I'd love to.''

Ethan couldn't believe how easy this was going to be. ''I imagine you could find a temporary job if you wanted one. Maybe not teaching, but something to do with kids. People are always looking for qualified nannies. Hey…'' He tried to sound as if the idea were just now occurring to him. ''Would you be interested in working for me? Just temporarily. I'm going to have to hire someone to watch Sallie and Alex until I get through this Merritt mediation, anyway. It'll last two, three days a week at most.…'' He gave her an assessing look. ''Maybe we can work out an arrangement. Something mutually beneficial.''

Her chin came up, fast. ''What *kind* of arrangement?''

She obviously recognized a proposition when

she heard one. Except she surely understood that this wasn't *that* sort of proposition. "This could work out great," he said, as if the idea were blooming piece by piece in his mind. "You'd get to see New York, Sallie and Alex wouldn't have to put up with the Millers, and I'd be able to concentrate completely on the Merritt settlement."

"Millers?" Libby questioned. "Merritt settlement? Are you a lawyer?"

"Yes, but not a practicing attorney. I work as a negotiator. When a company has a contract dispute with its employees, I'm called in as one of a team of consultants. The Merritt Hotel chain is involved in such a dispute at this very minute."

"And you're going to resolve it?"

"I'm going to give it my best shot."

"Do you represent the employers or the employees?"

"I represent the middle ground. With me, everyone wins or the deal never gets off the table."

"Hmm. So, who are the Millers?"

"They're the elderly couple who baby-sit Sallie and Alex when, for one reason or another, the nanny can't."

"What happened to your nanny?"

"She stayed in Rome to marry her one true love."

"Oooh," Libby said, a new interest lighting her eyes. "The plot thickens. Is she the reason you've sworn off women and romance?"

"Neesa? Hardly. I think she's crazy to marry a guy she barely knows, but there was never anything remotely romantic between the two of us. She was my employee, nothing more. Even if there had been something else—which I assure you, there wasn't—it wouldn't have any bearing on our arrangement. Yours and mine. So, I guess the question is, Libby, are you interested in a temporary position taking care of Sallie and Alex?"

She met his gaze and a little jolt of awareness rippled across his consciousness. For the first time, Ethan considered the possibility that this could become more complicated than he anticipated. Except that he wasn't about to let that happen. Libby was young, pretty, good with his kids, and under no circumstances was he going to be attracted to her. Period. Therefore, there would be no complications and that meant he had absolutely no reason to worry.

On the other hand, it couldn't hurt to spell things out. "In exchange for watching the kids, I'll provide you with a place to stay, all you can eat, a small salary and the perfect excuse to see everything New York City has to offer. Broadway shows. Radio City Music Hall. Art galleries. Museums. Restaurants. Delis. All the tourist attractions. The whole experience.''

She shook her head sadly. ''Even with a small salary and no living expenses, I couldn't afford the New York experience. I'd end up flat broke, instead of nearly so.''

''I meant that I'd pay for *all* expenses, Libby. Tickets, souvenirs, spending money, everything. I can afford it.''

Her brows dropped into a frown. ''Negotiating contracts must be a lot more lucrative than it sounds.''

She didn't beat around the bush, that was for sure. Ethan rather liked her forthrightness and decided to return it in kind. ''Business is good, but I work because I like it, not because I have to. I inherited a substantial trust fund when I turned twenty-five. Then when my mother died, there was insurance and the rest of my father's estate. I'm not Bill Gates, but I can afford to finance a tour of New York City in exchange for your help with the kids.''

''If Grampa George were here, he'd accuse you of 'pulling my leg like I was nothing but taffy.'''

Ethan smiled. "Look, Libby, I don't make a practice of telling people my business or offering all-expense paid trips to strangers. I need your help. Sallie doesn't put her faith in many people, and the fact that she trusts you means you're someone special. Believe me, this is a win-win proposition for all of us."

"Unless Alex and Sallie hate sightseeing."

She was going to do it. Ethan nearly said a triumphant, *Yes!* "They'll like anything that isn't watching television with the Millers."

Libby looked doubtful. "You think they'll like visiting museums and the Statue of Liberty and the Empire State Building and stuff like that?"

"Trust me, they'll love it," he said, not knowing how they'd feel about spending the rest of the week in sightseeing activities, not caring much either. They liked Libby. They'd adjust. "Sounds like a perfect arrangement to me."

"Perfect." She repeated the word slowly, as if the idea alone was a loophole. "You're offering me an expenses-paid vacation in New York City, plus a salary, and all you want me to do is watch your kids while you work? That's it?"

"Yes. What else could there be?"

She eyed him thoughtfully, making him the

slightest bit uncomfortable. "No hidden agendas? No after-the-kids-are-in-bed duties?"

He smiled, as if the thought were ridiculous…which, of course, it was. "I've sworn off romance, remember? So have you. There won't be any after-hours expectations, I assure you." He paused. "I can supply you with character references, if you're worried."

"I'm not worried," she said. "But you probably ought to know that I have three brothers and a bunch of rowdy male cousins. What I didn't learn from fighting with them, I picked up in the karate lessons my father insisted I take before I could start dating. Should the need arise, I know how to take care of myself."

He raised an eyebrow, half surprised by her statement, half amused she felt it necessary to tell him. "Karate? Hmm. Well, in that case, forget about taking care of the kids. I'll hire you to protect me from the big, bad city." He smiled, so she'd know he was teasing her again. "If I had any doubts before, you just cleared them up for me. The last thing I need in my life is a woman who can't take care of herself. So, Ms. Waldron, for a lot of reasons, I believe this could work out beneficially for both of us. Do we have a deal?"

Chapter Four

What a deal this was turning out to be, Libby thought as she walked through the lobby of the Plaza Hotel and tried not to gawk. She'd seen the hotel in pictures, read about it in books, watched its elegance blur into the background of movies, and never, ever imagined it was so grand. Revolving doors in gleaming brass, high ceilings, glittering chandeliers, red carpets that looked well trod but not worn, dark, richly oiled wood, luxurious details—everything in the hotel seemed to extend an invitation to come inside and be pampered. Doormen and clerks greeted her with a smile and Ethan by name. "Good evening, Mr. Redwine. Welcome back to New York. Hello, Sallie. Alex."

"Hi, Simon! Hello, Mr. Derck!" Alex and Sallie seemed quite at home here, and Libby took it all in in a soft blur of sound, color and impression. The Plaza. She was going to spend a few days at the Plaza. She'd spend them working—if playing with Sallie and Alex could be called work—but still she was here. In New York City. A place she'd never thought she would see. Rome. New York. For someone who'd never been out of Texas, she was suddenly quite the world traveler.

"I'D PLANNED TO MOVE OUT to Long Island, but the house deal fell through at the last minute, so the kids and I will be staying at the Plaza for the time being." Ethan turned on a light, giving Libby a glimpse of another hotel room, a smaller one, next door to the suite where Alex and Sallie were even now making themselves at home. "We stayed here for a couple of months after I sold our condo and before the Italy trip, so the kids are used to living in the hotel. It's not home, but it's not bad. At least you'll be able to tell the folks back in Beauregarde that you did New York in style."

"This is nice" was all she could think to say, even though living in a hotel sounded almost decadently luxurious.

"Yes, it is nice." Ethan smiled and stepped aside to let her enter. "I'm going to order pizza for the kids and I'd love for you to join us. If you're not too tired.''

"I've never felt better,'' Libby said, wanting to hug herself and laugh aloud. But she tried not to look as impressed as she was. "And I love pizza. As soon as I've freshened up a bit, I'll be over.''

"Great,'' Ethan said. "Perfect.'' He left, closing the door behind him and leaving Libby to luxuriate in her very own room at the premier hotel of New York City, leaving her to wonder if a deal this good could possibly be for real.

"MORE THTORY, PLEATHE.'' Sallie yawned into Libby's arm but resolutely kept her eyelids up as she tapped the book. "More *Poky Little Puppy*.''

"Oh, come on, Sallie,'' Alex complained. "You've already heard that dumb book three times. Libby doesn't want to read it again. She wants to play another game of Donkey Kong Land with me.''

Sallie looked at her brother, then lifted anxious eyes to Libby. "More, pleathe?''

"I'll read it one more time.'' Libby nestled the little girl into the curve of her arm. "Then we're turning off the lights. Alex, I promise tomorrow morning, first thing, we'll play a game of Donkey

Kong Land. I wouldn't be much competition for you tonight, anyway. Maybe in the morning I'll at least have a fair shot at beating you.''

Alex grinned and slumped down under the covers of his bed. ''You can't,'' he said, his fingers still moving across the game's keypad. ''You can try, but you can't beat me.''

Libby was a little intimidated at the ease with which these children had welcomed her into their nightly routine. They'd been happy to share their pizza with her. Happy to be tucked into bed by her. Happy to have her read their bedtime story. In fact, they seemed to accept her presence as easily as they'd accepted Ethan's quiet suggestion when it was time for bed.

He'd kissed them each good-night, hugged them soundly and returned to the laptop computer that had held his attention all evening. Libby had watched him covertly all the while she ate pizza with the kids, studying his strong features and trying to see if they were duplicated in any form in his children. They each had a distinctive ethnic heritage—Sallie was Eurasian, and Alex, Hispanic—but that heritage could have come from their respective mothers. The longer Libby studied the lines of Ethan's face, however, the more she doubted that his gene pool could be so overshadowed. The children were most likely adopted, which didn't explain where their adoptive mother was now or why they seemed to miss her so little. Whoever she was, whatever had happened to her, it was clear she'd been gone long enough that her absence went unnoticed in their daily routines.

Libby didn't quite know how to begin asking questions, but she knew she needed to know. Sallie had a definite lisp and a slight developmental delay in language skills, and Alex seemed very wrapped up in his video games—which might mean something, or nothing at all. Either way, Libby wasn't going to assume temporary responsibility for these two children without knowing more about them. Partly because she wanted to be prepared in case they asked her about their mother, and partly—mainly—because Ethan Redwine stirred her curiosity.

Stirrin' curiosity's worse than stirrin' a hornet's nest, Grampa George had told her thousands of times over the endless summers of her childhood. *With hornets,* he'd warned, *the worst that can happen is a few stings. With curiosity, there's no tellin' the trouble that'll swarm ya.*

But, as Libby had told Ethan, she knew how to take care of herself, even if no one in Beauregarde, Texas, believed her.

ETHAN LOOKED UP FROM the computer when Libby walked into the sitting area. Her hair was once again disheveled and wisped around and away from her face in an appealing lack of style. Her smile brought an answering curve to his lips, and just looking at her was the most pleasure he'd had in weeks. The thought brought him up short. He did not need complications, he reminded himself. He worked with attractive women all the time and never mixed business with pleasure. This was no different...and it was going to stay that way. No matter how pretty she was. "Are they asleep?" he asked, and she nodded.

"I'm amazed at how long they were able to stay awake." She glanced at her watch. "It's only seven-thirty here, but that's two-thirty in the morning in Rome."

"They've traveled a lot," he offered as explanation. "They're used to coping with jet lag."

"Jet lag," Libby repeated with a tiny frown. "You know, I was so excited going over I must have missed out on that experience. I don't feel a bit *lag-y* now, either, though, so maybe I'm immune."

"Flying west is always an easier adjustment than traveling east." Ethan focused again on the computer screen, just to keep from watching the myriad nuances of her expression. "Still, it's normal to be tired after a long flight."

"Well, I'm not. Tired, I mean. I feel great. In fact, if you don't mind, I think I'll stand here and look out your window for a little while. The view from my window isn't anything like this. Just another building. Wow. That must be..." She glanced back at him for confirmation. "Central Park?"

He nodded. "Central Park and Fifth Avenue."

"Really? Fifth Avenue? Like 'in your Easter bonnet' Fifth Avenue?"

His lips curved at the mention of such a golden oldie, but he hid the smile and simply nodded again. She resumed watching the busyness on the streets below...and he resumed watching her, noting the lovely alignment of her shoulders and slender neck as she turned her head from the Central Park view to get the Fifth Avenue perspective.

"Sure are a lot of people out there," she said a moment later, then a moment after that added, "I didn't know you could get carriage rides in New York City. Where do they go?"

"Central Park, mostly, although around Christmas, they'll take people as far as Rockefeller Center."

"Rockefeller Center," she repeated. "NBC studios, Katie, Matt and Al. I'd love to see that."

Ethan smiled at her "Today Show" rundown, wondering which one was the bigger draw, figuring the odds were good for Matt. "You should walk down there some morning."

"You mean, I can *walk* there from here?"

"Manhattan is a fraction of the size of Texas, Libby. You can walk nearly anywhere you want to go...providing you like to walk. From the Plaza, you could probably walk to Rockefeller Center in ten, fifteen minutes."

"Really?" She seemed thoroughly delighted with that little detail. As if seeing the NBC studios had been a lifelong dream of hers.

"If you get there early enough and wait long enough, you might even get a few seconds on camera to say hi to the folks back in Beauregarde."

"I'd just as soon Beauregarde didn't know I was here, thanks. Besides, I doubt Alex and Sallie would think the 'Today Show' was worth getting up early for."

"Why not?"

She glanced over her shoulder at him. "Would you get up early to stand outside in a crowd and wave to a TV camera?"

"No, but then I'm camera shy. And I was asking why you don't want your family and friends to know where you are."

She quickly turned back to the view. "They think I'm still in Rome, and I'm in no hurry for them to find out differently."

"Do they think you're with...the idiot?"

"They think I'm *married* to him. Or about to be, anyway."

Ethan's eyebrows rose. That was an unforeseen complication, for certain. "Oh," he said. "Are you?"

"Hardly," she said...and he was relieved. Extremely so. "It's the only way they'd let me get on the plane by myself." She paused. "Did I mention my family is a little overprotective of me?"

"Is that because you live in a small town?"

"No, it's because I'm the first female born into the Waldron family in three generations. The only female child, to date."

"And your overly protective family let you go to Italy *alone* to get married?"

"I didn't say they liked the idea. I sprang it on them at the last minute, and they didn't have time to do anything except fuss. I told them I was flying to Rome to meet his family and have a ceremony there and that then we'd come back together and have a Texas-style wedding with them.''

''But that wasn't what you planned originally?''

''Oh, no, it was just the best excuse I could think of on short notice. I was in something of a hurry to get out of town.''

''And you're in no hurry to go back?''

''I'm draggin' my feet like a centipede in rubber boots.''

He smiled at her droll tone. ''Now, if I've gotten this right, you left home and went to Rome because you believed you were going to marry this man, this…idiot. But when you got to Rome, you found out otherwise. There wasn't a ceremony there, and the wedding in Texas isn't going to happen, either.'' Ethan made it a statement and not a question, although he didn't know why that seemed important.

''Oh, I'm not sure I believed it ever was going to happen. I was sort of…overwhelmed with circumstances.''

''Circumstances?''

Her hand moved in a wide, random circle. ''Oh, you know, I lost my job and my apartment and everyone insisted that going to the football game would cheer me up, and then there was the marriage proposal, and, well, Rome suddenly seemed like a great idea. Then I got to Rome and it wasn't such a great idea, either.''

''Wait. Marriage proposal?''

She nodded. ''At half time. The marching band spelled out the words *Marry me, Libby.*''

Ethan frowned. He'd been so sure he had the whole thing figured out. ''So, he'd already *met* your family when he proposed?''

''Jason Joe?'' Libby frowned back. ''He's known my family forever. We grew up together.''

''So why did you go to Rome?''

''For Nick's birthday.''

''And who's Nick?''

''The one in bed with the brunette.''

''I thought you went to marry him.''

''I thought so, too.'' Her attention wandered back to the window.

Ethan decided he was going to get this straight, one way or the other. ''Okay, who is Jason Joe?''

''He's the one who proposed to me during half time at the football game. He's one of the coaches.''

''How many proposals of marriage were there?''

''In my whole life? Or just this week?''

"Let's take it a month at a time," he suggested, not entirely sure she was kidding.

"Three, this month. Well, really, only one, because the baggage man at the airport wasn't serious and Nick obviously didn't mean what I thought he meant when he invited me to his villa."

"For his birthday," Ethan supplied, as if that summed it all up nicely.

"He said he hated to spend his birthday alone, but as it turned out, there was a four-point spread between his idea of alone and mine."

"That's where the brunette came in."

"Two brunettes and a redhead. I was the token blonde."

That was so patently ridiculous, Ethan wanted to laugh aloud, but he settled for a you're-kidding-me lift of his brow. "Pardon me if I find that a little hard to believe."

"What? That he had one of each shade? Oh, you can believe it. We were all in that bedroom together. Four women to one lice. Louse." Her hand moved in a dismissive wave as her attention was drawn back to the view. "I shouldn't have been so naive and impulsive in the first place. I, obviously, imagined some emotions that weren't there to begin with."

"On his part?" Ethan asked. "Or yours?"

"Mmm. There goes one of the carriages. Funny, I'd swear I can hear the sound of the horse's hooves on the pavement. Would Alex and Sallie like that, do you think? Taking a carriage ride in the park? Or are they so accustomed to it, they'd think it wasn't any fun?"

Ethan closed the laptop, finally admitting there was no point in pretending an interest in anything other than Libby. "They'd think it was fun. Sallie adores the carriage horses. In fact, I suppose those are the only horses she's ever seen."

"She should see the horses on my brother's ranch. My uncle Hoot has horses, too, and dozens of cows. My cousin, Juner, even has a pair of llamas."

"Really?" Ethan had an incongruous image of a cowboy lassoing a llama. "They spit, don't they?" he asked.

"Only if you let them chew tobacco."

There was a pause, a beat, before Libby looked back at him with a saucy smile and he realized she was teasing. He didn't have a choice...he smiled back. "I heard they have a nasty attitude, too."

"Well, Uncle Hoot has his moments, but my brother and cousin are usually pretty nice guys."

Ethan was more than a little fascinated by the coy amusement in her tone. "What about the llamas?"

"Are you kidding? They're in seventh heaven on Juner's ranch. He fawns over them as if he didn't have a lick of good sense."

"I must have been misinformed about the attitude of llamas."

She wrinkled her nose. "I didn't say I *liked* them. They do have a lousy attitude and they do spit. But just because an animal exhibits unattractive behaviors doesn't mean they don't contribute something of benefit to the world. I try to keep in mind that all of God's creatures are good for something."

"That's a lovely sentiment."

"I love animals," she answered simply. "All of them. Well, almost all of them. I'm not crazy about llamas, for sure, and I wouldn't want a rat for a pet. Or an alligator. But I don't really count reptiles as animals, even though, I guess, technically, they are. I love practically every other kind of pet, though. At home, I have three dogs, two cats, a parakeet, a chameleon, four goldfish and a whole passel of banty chickens."

"Don't tell Sallie or she'll demand to see them. Immediately, if not sooner."

"She and Alex don't have a pet?"

He shook his head. Firmly.

Libby was openly disappointed. "It must be difficult to keep a pet in a city like this."

"It's hard to keep one anywhere, but the city is more inconvenient. Although, there are a lot of people in New York City who have pets."

"But not you."

"I have no need for one."

"Alex and Sallie do."

"They don't. As I said, they've traveled a lot. There hasn't been much time for the care and up-keep of a pet."

"I think we ought to talk about that," she said, and Ethan scooted his chair away from the desk and stood.

"There's nothing to talk about," he said. "We're not getting a pet of any kind and that's definite."

She stopped darting glances out the window and faced him, giving her chin a brave little lift. "That isn't what I meant, although I can't imagine kids without pets. They're therapeutic, you know."

"Kids?"

"Pets."

"Oh, yes, kids and pets." He didn't want to

know why she thought his kids needed a pet, because he wasn't budging on the issue. Not even a quarter inch. "So what was it you wanted to talk about? Salary?"

"Salary?" she echoed. "No, of course not." Her lips curved with a sudden bright and breathtaking smile. "But don't get the wrong idea. Having a paycheck is always good and I am interested in what you intend to pay me. But I'm not concerned about it. Getting to stay here for a few days is like a paid vacation, anyway. Plus, it'll give me a little time to figure out what I'm going to say to the folks back home." She frowned, hesitated, then inhaled sharply. "No, what I thought we should talk about was…*is*…Alex and Sallie. I'd like to know about them. About their… background and, well, anything else that might be pertinent."

"Pertinent?" But he knew what she wanted to know, what everyone seemed to ask, sooner or later. "The story of their adoptions, you mean."

Libby folded her hands at her waist and nodded. "And about their mother, too. If I'm going to be spending time with them, the subject is bound to come up, and I don't want to say or do something that will upset them. Or you."

He wished he could deny that she had a valid

point, a legitimate interest. It was just that so
many people felt they had a right to know. Adoption, he'd learned, was seldom, if ever private.
"There isn't much to tell. Alex was two years old
when I found him, abandoned, in Guatemala and
decided I was going to adopt him. It took another
year and a half before all the paperwork was finished and I could bring him to the States. Sallie
was born in this country. She was three weeks old
when I brought her home. Her mother was an
exchange student from China, interning in our office. She knew she couldn't keep her baby and
knew about Alex's adoption, so she asked me if
I wanted to adopt Sallie, too. In both cases, I was
lucky. I knew someone who could handle the red
tape and I happened to be in the right place at the
right time."

Libby looked at him with disconcerting frankness. "What about their adoptive mother? Your
wife?"

"Ex-wife," he corrected her, with feeling.
"Diane said she wanted children and seemed enthusiastic about adoption, but somehow she just
never bonded with the children. Said she hadn't
expected them to be so...different, whatever that
meant. Just after Sallie turned three, Diane called
me at the office to say she was leaving. By the

time I got home, she was gone. On her way to Italy with a man she claimed was her *true* love. I didn't even know she'd been having an affaire.''

"I'm sorry," Libby said simply.

Ethan shrugged an indifference that had been a long time coming. "Looking back, I realize I should have seen the signs and recognized how unhappy she was, but at the time I thought everything was fine and would continue to be so.''

Her smile was gentle. "I'm a pretty good Monday morning quarterback, myself. I should have recognized Nick was too charming, too handsome, too *everything* to love just one woman. And I should have realized what Jason Joe was up to before he got hold of the microphone and said, 'Well, Libby, how 'bout it?''' She shook her head in sad amusement. "I mean, I should have figured it out first quarter, when he…'' She stopped. "I'm sorry. I do that sometimes. Rattle on about something when I don't know what else to say. I wasn't trying to compare my silly love triangle with your wife abandoning you and your kids, at all.''

"Ex-wife," he corrected her again, but without as much emphasis.

"But not ex-mother.''

"No, unfortunately.'' Ethan stuck his hands in

his pockets and moved closer to her, until he, too, could see the view of Central Park and Fifth Avenue. "The problem is, I just don't know how much she's going to be in their lives." He hadn't meant to tell her any of this, but suddenly he needed to tell someone...and Libby was listening. "Diane called once a week for the first two months after she left, then more sporadically as time passed. Then she showed up, with new husband, Roberto, and wanted to be a mother after all, said she missed Alex and Sallie.

"For a month, she drove me crazy, wrecked our routines, kept the kids later than she'd said she would, or brought them back sooner than expected, told them she was never leaving them again, then left...again. Then nothing. No word at all for several months, then, presto, she was back to do it all over again. I tried to protect them, tried to be the generous custodial parent, tried talking to her, tried to keep as much stability in their lives as I could, but all the time, I was paranoid that she was going to call me from Italy one afternoon to say she'd taken them home with her. But instead, she called one morning."

"She took them to another country, without your knowledge?"

He nodded. "I retrieved them and told her to

get her head straight before she started pretending to be a mother again. There was no word from her for nearly six months after that. Then, suddenly, she was calling, apologizing all over the place, telling me how wrong she'd been, begging me to bring the kids for a visit. So we went...and that seemed to go really well. Then she came to New York for a week and that went well, too. When she asked if Alex and Sallie could go home with her, I refused, but she persisted and the kids wanted to go. I'd sold the condo, anticipating our move to Long Island, and when the house deal fell through, I reconsidered her request. Sallie isn't in school yet and Alex attends a private school that's on a twelve-month schedule. He was out for a month, I had business in Paris, and a few days with Diane sounded like it might be a nice little vacation for them. Plus, I finally had an employee I trusted implicitly to watch out for the kids' best interests."

"Neesa," Libby said, supplying the name. "The nanny who stayed in Rome to marry her one true love."

His smile curved without humor. "She'd been working for me for nearly a year and I had a lot of faith in her judgment. Sallie was crazy about

Neesa, but the feeling obviously wasn't mutual, because I couldn't persuade Neesa to reconsider.''

"They're not her kids," Libby suggested. "You surely didn't expect her to give up her own dreams for marriage and a family."

"I expected her to watch my children, instead of leaving them with Roberto's decrepit old father while she and Diane kept secret rendezvous with Antonio and his brother. I happened to phone one afternoon, and when Alex said he hadn't seen his mother in a couple of days and that Neesa hadn't been around much, either, I cut short my business in Paris and doubled back to pick up the kids. Believe me, it was not a pretty scene, and if I have anything to say about it, none of us are setting foot in Italy again."

"I'm surprised you even tried to persuade Neesa to stay on as nanny after that."

He'd been afraid that losing Neesa would send Sallie into a tailspin, and until Libby rescued her at the airport, it had. But he didn't want to say that, not here, not now. "To be honest, I blame myself for the situation. I knew how charmingly irresponsible Diane was. If I'd thought about it for half a second, I'd have realized Neesa was too young and inexperienced to stand up to her."

"How could you have anticipated a situation like that?" Libby asked.

"How could I *not* have? I'm their father. It's my job to protect them at all costs."

"I think you're being too hard on yourself, especially since everything worked out okay. You have them home again. No harm done. Lighten up, Ethan. I'll tell you what I tell my preschool parents—what I *used* to tell them, anyway, when I had a job. And the advice is—relax, enjoy your kids and do the best job of parenting you can. If you're going to worry about everything that can go wrong, nothing is going to go right."

He looked at her, thinking how beautifully simple her advice was, how wonderful it would be to believe it. "Did you pick up that philosophy in Beauregarde, Texas?" he asked with a slow smile.

"You bet," she answered, matching the smile. "That and so many other down-home remedies it'd make your head whirl. My grampa George is quite a philosopher."

"What did Grampa George tell you about going to Rome?"

She made a face. A fascinating moue of an expression. "He said I could get spaghetti at home."

Ethan laughed. So did Sallie, who'd walked, unnoticed, into the room. "I want pthgetti," she said, a happy smile wreathing her little, round face as she lifted her arms to Libby.

"What are you doing out of bed?" With a tender curving of her lips, Libby picked Sallie up and hugged her. Ethan noticed that his daughter hugged back...and in that instant of watching Libby's white-blond curls fall across Sallie's blue-black hair, he had an idea.

A bad idea.

A really bad idea.

Still, if there was any way it might work...

No, he thought. Forget it. Sallie will be okay without a mother. She'll be okay without Neesa. She'll be okay.

But he couldn't help thinking how much better she already was with Libby.

Chapter Five

"Daddy, look!" Sallie scampered like a rabbit up and down the sidewalk, pointing to each carriage horse in turn. "That one ith Barney, an' that one ith Maythee, an' that ith Jingle, and that one—" Her finger wavered at the fourth horse and she turned to Libby. "I can't 'member."

"Miss Kitty," Libby prompted.

"Mith Kitty," Sallie repeated, resuming the recital and the pointing. "An' that one ith Bob, an' that one ith Frothty—like the thnowman—and that one way down there ith…"

Again, she glanced at Libby, who prompted, "Gladys."

Then again the wide smile that Ethan still couldn't quite believe was coming from his daughter. "Gladyth," Sallie repeated, nodding her head with infinite satisfaction.

Ethan scooped her into his arms and hugged her. "That was wonderful, Sallie. You have a terrific memory."

She pushed against him, beaming as she cupped his face in her little hands. "I do, Daddy. Libby thaid I'm a terrific 'memerererer."

"You're just terrific all over," he said, and nuzzled her neck until she giggled...a sound he'd heard too seldom in her short life. When Sallie wriggled free to stand independently on the sidewalk and admire the horses, Ethan held on to her hand and wondered what had come over his shy, quiet daughter. Then he turned his head to look closely at Libby.

"What?" she asked, catching the inquiry in his gaze.

"You taught Sallie how to giggle."

Libby's delicate eyebrows rose. "You can't blame me for that. She was born knowing how."

"Then thanks for helping her *'member.*"

"Oh. You're welcome, although I don't think I had much to do with it. She's very happy to see you."

He'd been buried under the Merritt Hotel dispute for the last three days, but now it was settled, a done deal, and his schedule was clear for the immediate future. An autoworkers' union was threatening a strike, but it hadn't happened yet, might not happen at all, and Ethan was free to enjoy a few days with his children. And Libby. Fascinating, captivating Libby, who had somehow coaxed an afternoon's worth of giggles from his daughter.

Sallie tugged on his hand again. "Com'ere, Daddy. Com'ere."

He let her lead him down the sidewalk, listening intently as she told him all the horse's names again. As they made the return trip to where Libby and Alex waited, Ethan noticed the conspiratorial look his son exchanged with her and was suddenly aware that there wasn't a Game Boy in sight. Or hand. Now, how had she accomplished that?

"Dad?" Alex shifted from one foot to the other, his eyes anxious and hopeful. "Libby said if it was okay with you that Travis could spend the night. Is it okay, Dad? Is it?"

Ethan laid his hand on his son's head. "We're sort of crowded at the hotel, son. Maybe it would be better to wait until we move to—" Libby cleared her throat…meaningfully…and Ethan read the advice in her raised eyebrows. She was right. No telling when he'd find another house. Or when they'd move. And Alex needed the company of his peers now. "Sure, son. I see no reason Travis shouldn't spend the night. Just so long as you promise me the two of you won't stay up all night playing video games."

"We won't, Dad. We won't, I promise. Can I call him now? Can I, Dad?"

Ethan tuned into the traffic and city noise for a second. "Now?" he questioned. "Here?"

"I can use your cell phone, Dad. He's waitin' for me to call him…and I've got his number right here. I wrote it down." Alex proudly held up his hand to display the seven digits inked onto his palm.

"You wrote a phone number on your hand?"

Alex nodded an eager agreement. "Libby said her nephews always write down stuff on their hands, so I did, too. It's a bunch easier than findin' a piece of paper to write somethin' on." He turned his palm so he could admire his own efficiency. "That's a way cool idea, huh, Dad?"

"Oh, yeah, *way* cool." His glance traveled back to Libby. "Please tell me he didn't use permanent ink."

She made a face. "We'll hope not, but there's no guarantee. I told him about the time one of my nephews wrote his spelling words on his hand so he wouldn't have to study, and then he couldn't get the ink to wash off. For about two months, he was walking around with the words *genius, brilliant, trustworthy* and *cleanliness,* written on his palm. All, unfortunately, misspelled.''

Ethan laughed and handed his cell phone into Alex's outstretched hand, wondering again how Libby had managed not only to take Neesa's place in his children's affection, but also to work this miracle of a transformation in their attitudes. He didn't really care. Didn't want to know if she'd threatened, cajoled or simply expected them to turn off the tears and turn on the smiles.

All that mattered to him was the tenuous trust he saw in his children's dark eyes. All he cared about was the happy anticipation that seemed to have settled in their expressions. All he hoped was that this new phase of childhood was going to last and that Libby would be around for a very long time.

The idea returned in all its inherent complexity, still bad, still a thought that deserved to be banished from his brain. Yet, with each recurrence, the whole idea didn't seem quite as bad as before. Not that he was actually considering it. Marrying Libby to ensure that she would stick around for a good long while was a bad idea. A really bad, terrible, awful idea. It wasn't fair. Or honest. Or right.

Just incredibly persistent.

"I HAVE AN IDEA," Ethan said when Sallie had dragged him up and down the row of carriage horses until he could repeat the litany of their names in his sleep. "Let's take Libby to the Empire State Building. I don't think she's ever seen it."

"We went there yesterday," Alex informed him. "Besides, Travis is supposed to be here any minute. We'd better wait right here."

"Travis's mother said she'd bring him to the hotel at seven-thirty. That's three hours from now. Libby's never been to New York before, and I think we ought to show her some of the sights."

"We did, Daddy," Sallie said. "We thowed 'er all everything."

Ethan looked down at his bright-eyed daughter. "All that, huh? And you're sure there's not a single sight you missed? Did you ride the carousel in Central Park? See the Statue of Liberty? Walk down Fifth Avenue in your Easter bonnet?"

Sallie's head stopped bobbing agreement and turned upward. "Did we, Libby?"

"We did everything except the bonnet," Libby

assured her, then for clarity, added, "That means we didn't wear hats."

Sallie's frown disappeared like magic as she turned back to Ethan. "No hatth!" she announced happily.

"Tell me this." Ethan bent to Sallie's level, pretending his question was for her and not Libby. "Did you get up early one morning to see the 'Today Show' and Matt Lauer?"

"No, we did not." Libby frowned down at him. "We stayed a good long ways from Rockefeller Center and any television cameras roaming the city."

He nodded, pleased for no good reason he could think of. "In that case, let's walk down there. We can look in the NBC window when there's no chance of getting caught on camera."

"No chance?"

"None. Not at this time of day." He rose and leaned close to whisper, "Please say yes. If I have to name these horses one more time, I'm going to have night-*mares*."

"Funny," she said, and he breathed in the scent of...bubble gum? He leaned closer for another sniff.

She turned her head at the same moment, and her face was suddenly and tantalizingly close to his. Awareness fell like a snowflake against his skin, fragile, fascinating and fleeting.

"What?" she asked, reclaiming her space with a tilt of her head. "Do I need a breath mint?"

Ethan straightened slowly, reluctantly. "No. I thought I smelled...bubble gum."

"Oh, no." Her hand went to her hair. "Sallie's gum got stuck in my hair this afternoon. I thought I'd cut it out, but maybe I didn't get it all. Is it noticeable?"

All he could see was the heavy white-gold strands of her hair as she held them up and let them fall in a wispy shower that formed those odd and attractive little sprouts around her face. "My daughter put bubble gum in your hair?"

"It was an accident," Libby said quickly. "My hair was in the wrong place at the wrong time." She smiled down at Sallie. "But we handled it, didn't we, Sal?"

"I blew bubbleth," Sallie said proudly. "Big bubbleth. Alex did, too. But Libby blew the big-geth of all."

Ethan wasn't sure that was something to brag about, but it obviously had impressed his kids. And if it made them happy, he was for it a hundred percent. Well, seventy-five percent, anyway.

"None of my teachers ever encouraged gum chewing."

Libby lifted one shoulder in an intriguing little shrug. "Did that stop you?"

"As a matter of fact, yes."

Her lips formed a curve he wanted to pay attention to, but Alex chose that moment to tug on his sleeve. "When's he going to get here, Dad? How much longer before Travis's mom drops him off?"

Definitely time for a distraction, Ethan decided. "He'll be here ten minutes after we get back."

"Where're we going?" Alex asked.

"Rockefeller Center."

"HI, HOW'RE YOU?"

Ethan's gaze followed Libby's greeting to a woman with a sour expression, who brushed past with a terse reply. "Who was that?" he asked, surprised that she would meet an acquaintance on Fifth Avenue.

"I don't know." Libby turned her head to look after the woman. "Do you think she's someone famous?"

"No. I just thought perhaps you knew her."

"No." Libby smiled and nodded to a man coming toward them at a brisk pace. "Hello," she said pleasantly. The man glanced at her but never slowed his pace. "Do you know him?" Ethan asked.

She shook her head, still smiling, her gaze bouncing from one face to the next. "Hi, there. How are you?"

Another woman passed, maintaining her get-out-of-my-way, I'm-in-a-hurry, New York stride. "Hello. Hi." Libby graced two more passersby with her cheery accent and Texas smile.

Stopping the kids with one hand, Ethan pulled Libby out of the flow of sidewalk traffic. "What are you doing?" he asked her.

Her brow furrowed. "What?"

"Talking to everyone you meet."

"I'm not talking to them. I'm just being friendly."

"Libby, this isn't Texas."

"What difference does that make? Friendly is friendly, no matter where you are."

"Not exactly." He looked past her to the people walking by and wondered how to explain that friendly was a subjective concept and that her small-town idea of "friendly" could get her into trouble in the Big Apple. "In this city, we don't say hello to everyone we pass on the sidewalk."

"Why not?"

Why not? He tried to think of a way to explain the difference. "It, uh, well, it's just not the thing to do."

"It's not the thing to do," she repeated with a frown, then strung her follow-up into an elongated question. "Because…?"

"Because…it could be suspicious."

"Suspicious?" Her frown cleared, replaced by a look of delightful amusement. "Saying hello to people is *suspicious?*"

It sounded ridiculous put like that, but he didn't know how to explain it any better. "Look, just take my word for it, okay? No one's going to answer you, anyway."

She just looked at him, her eyes so clear and blue a man could drown in them. "Well, thanks, Ethan, for warning me. I'd hate to seem *suspicious.* How many more blocks to Rockefeller Center?"

He checked the storefront behind them, relieved that she'd accepted his advice in the spirit in which it was meant. "We're nearly there. It's just a little over two blocks from here."

Her chin dipped in a nod as she gathered Sallie's hand into her own. "Then what are we waiting for? Let's go."

Alex was engrossed in the Halloween display

in the store window, and Ethan had to take his shoulders and turn him face front before they could resume their walk. Libby fell into step beside him, with Sallie and Alex between.

"Hello," Libby said not even half a block later to a woman approaching them at a steady clip. "How are you?"

The woman's expression transformed with surprise and pleasure. "I'm fine, thanks," she said as she passed Libby. "How are you?"

"Fine, thanks," Libby replied as Ethan's frown met its match in her cheerful smile. This time, he just kept walking.

"OH, LOOK! SOMEBODY dropped a wallet!"

Before he could grab her, Libby dashed forward and picked up the small red billfold. Ethan looked around, hoping no one was watching, hoping no one was hauling a policeman across the street to arrest whoever had stolen their wallet...because Libby had it in her hand and was riffling through the contents and looked as highly suspicious as it was possible for a blonde with innocent blue eyes to look.

"I wish you hadn't done that," Ethan muttered as she walked toward him and the kids with a smile as wide as Broadway.

"Done what?" she asked, counting the money inside. "One dollar and twenty-seven cents. Can you believe it? Some poor soul is walking around New York City unaware that they've just lost their last dollar and twenty-seven cents."

"Some pickpocket is probably walking around with the other thousand."

Libby glanced at him. "That doesn't make sense. If you're going to rob somebody, then you'd take it all. Why would a thief leave a dollar and twenty-seven cents?"

"Maybe he has a kind heart."

"I'm sticking with my theory."

"Which is...?" Ethan had to ask, had to know how she was going to resolve the unknowns of the wallet. Even though he'd have preferred for her to drop the wallet back where she'd found it and move on.

"Which is that someone—" She opened a snap and pulled out a driver's license. "Mia Metts," she read, "dropped her wallet just a couple of minutes ago. It probably fell out of her purse, and now poor Mia, from Schenectady, New York, is walking around New York City without her last dollar and twenty-seven cents."

"And unaware that you're walking around *with* it."

Libby frowned. "You're right. I'd better try to find her phone number and leave a message that I've found her wallet. I'd hate for her to be worried about losing her license and credit cards and pictures. Oh, look..." Libby tucked the license back into its slot and pulled out a plastic photo folder. "Maybe Mia has a baby. See how sweet?" She held out the picture of a plump, bald infant for Ethan to see.

"Or maybe Mia *is* a baby," he commented.

"Don't be silly. Then she couldn't have a driver's license, could she?" Libby replaced everything and closed the wallet. "Is there a public phone around here someplace?"

"I don't suppose I could talk you into just mailing it to the address on her license, could I?"

She lifted an eyebrow, and with a nod, Ethan took her elbow and guided her toward a nearby café. "Au Bon Pain is right over here. There's a pay phone inside."

"Great," she said. "I hope I have enough change to make a long distance call. How much do you think it'll cost to call Schenectady?"

Ethan pulled out his wallet and handed over his calling card. "Use this. It'll be my contribution to the cause. The kids and I will go right over there and order some sandwiches while you're being the Good Samaritan. Do you want something?"

"Yes," she said. "I'll have whatever you're having. Thanks."

"You're welcome," he replied. When she looked up at him, all eyes and smile and generous spirit, something friendly and delightful wrapped around his heart.

"YOU'RE NEVER GOING TO believe this." Libby slid into the chair next to Alex and across from Ethan, her smile...impossibly...wider and brighter than before. "We have tickets to see *The Lion King*...if we want them."

Ethan set down his coffee cup. "Libby, don't tell me you used Mia's dollar and twenty-seven cents to buy theater tickets."

His teasing roused her dimple and made his effort worthwhile. "No, smarty pants. Even in Beauregarde, we know it costs seventy times that much for a Broadway show. I called information and got a phone number for Mia's address in upstate New York and talked to her mom, and guess what? Mia's an actress and she's in—"

"Let me guess...*Phantom of the Opera.*"

"Right!" Libby nodded enthusiastically, then stopped. "No, *The Lion King*. Anyway, her mother gave me the phone number that rings backstage and the first person who answered the phone couldn't believe I'd call to return a—"

"Dollar and twenty-seven cents," Ethan suggested.

"Wallet," Libby finished. "He was so impressed, he called someone else to the phone and I told them I wanted to return it, and while I talked to that person, somebody called Mia to the phone and she didn't even know the wallet was missing. She said if I'd bring it to the theater, she'd show me around backstage, and then somebody else got on the line and said I could have two tickets for tomorrow's matinee, if I wanted them."

"I hope you said yes."

She smiled excitedly. "Yes." Then the smile dimmed. "But I didn't feel I could ask for an extra ticket, and since Alex and Sallie can't go by themselves, maybe you could tell me where I can buy another ticket, so I can take them?"

"I'll do better than that. I'll get two extra and go with you." He paused, surprised by the anticipatory thrill that raced through him at the thought of sitting next to Libby in a dark theater. "Unless...you wanted to invite someone else."

"Oh, no. You're perfect," she said, then made

a wry face. "I mean, I'm glad you want to go with us."

"I wouldn't miss it for the world," he said, and meant it.

THE PLAZA LIGHTS BEAMED a welcome as Libby and Ethan shepherded two excited children up the steps and into the hotel lobby. "I can't get over the way those costumes made the actors seem like real animals," Libby said. "Didn't you think Mia *was* a lioness?"

"Yeah," Alex said, his ever-present Game Boy forgotten for the afternoon. "But I liked Scar better than anybody. He was real mean. If I was an actor, I'd want to be him."

Sallie jumped from one step to the next. "I want to be Mia. Did you like Mia, Dad? Did you like her betht?"

"I did, Sallie. I liked Mia best of all. Even more than Simba."

"I liked him, too," Sallie agreed. "Did you like him, too, Libby?"

"Yes. But I liked when Mia sang more than anything else."

"She was very good," Ethan agreed. "And she has a voice that's certainly powerful enough to belong to a lion. Incredible."

Libby smiled up at him, still caught up in the magic of live theater, still nearly as keyed up as Sallie and Alex, still wondering if she ought to pinch herself and make sure she was actually walking into the Plaza Hotel with the most considerate, most attentive, most attractive employer she could ever imagine. ''Now, aren't you glad I found that wallet?''

His slow smile could have stopped a train in its tracks. Little wonder, it made her heart skip a beat. ''I am more glad than I can say, Libby Waldron, that Sallie and Alex…and *I*…found you.''

It was a romantic thing to say, and he said it in a romantic tone of voice, with a romantic glint in his green eyes, and Libby wished for a moment that he wasn't her employer at all. For a fleeting moment, she imagined what it would be like to be the woman he kissed goodbye in the morning and came home to at the end of the day. The woman he went to sleep with and awakened next to. The woman he made passionate love to and in whose ear he whispered a lifetime of romantic words. The woman who shared his life, his home, his children. The woman lucky enough to be Ethan's wife.

''Libby Ann?'' A familiar figure loomed in her

peripheral vision and grew larger as he approached. "Libby Ann Waldron?"

There was no place to run, nowhere to hide, so with a sinking heart, she turned to see the handsome, all-American face of Jason Joe Johnson. "Libby Ann," he repeated with a relieved grin and a determined nod. "I've come to take you home."

Chapter Six

"Jason Joe," Libby said, wishing she could fall through the polished floor of the Plaza Hotel. "What...what are you doing here?"

His smile revealed teeth as perfect as his confidence. "Your folks asked me to come and fetch you home safely." He held open his arms. "Now, don't go pretendin' you're not happy to see me. I know you better than that, Libby Ann. Come here and give me a big hug."

She had no intention of encouraging him, but his hand closed over hers and she was jerked off balance and into his embrace. So, instead of making a scene, she let him hug her, gave him a quick squeeze in return, then stepped back. Except she couldn't step back because he held on after she'd let go, keeping her hostage in the protective circle of his arms.

"You sure have had everybody worried," he said against her hair. "The whole town's been in one humongous panic ever since we found out you weren't in Rome."

She managed to put a little bit of distance between them, but couldn't seem to extricate her hands from his light but insistent grasp. "I was in Rome," she corrected him, with a degree of insistence. "I just…came back a little sooner than I'd expected to, that's all."

"Yeah, that's what we heard. After that guy, that Nick person, phoned to make sure you got home all right, things got pretty tense around Beauregarde, especially in the Waldron clan."

"Nick called?" she asked, amazed. "Nick Carlucci?"

"Yeah," Jason Joe agreed. "He was afraid you might have had trouble getting out of the country and wanted to make sure you got home okay. You can't imagine how relieved we all were to find out you'd come to your senses and decided not to marry that foreigner. I told your mom this little trip to Italy was just one of those impulsive, wild-hare notions you take into your pretty little head every now and again, just to show the rest of us you have a mind of your own. Everybody knows you never had any notion of marrying any man but me to begin with. We all figured you wouldn't be gone two days before you'd realize where you belong.'' His smile was prime Jason Joe, all flash and no film...but the flash was always blinding. ''It was just a question of when you'd come scurrying back, begging me to forgive and forget. And I've already done the forgivin', Libby Ann—even if I did tell your mom you'd have to say 'pretty-please.''' He moved to gather her close again, but this time Libby was ready for him and eluded his possessive hug.

''Nick called,'' she repeated, sorry she'd ever given that man her real name, much less her address and phone number, sorrier still that she'd ever dated Jason Joe Johnson. ''So how did you find me?''

''Oh, you know your mom. She was calling the airlines the minute that Italian—'' he pronounced it *eye-towel-yun* ''—hung up the phone. Once she found out where you'd gotten off the plane, she set out to call every cab company, every bus station and every hotel in the state, got a list of 'em from that cousin of yours who married the travel agent. What's his name?''

''Terry. His wife's named Terri, too.'' Libby felt a mix of frustration and admiration for the resourcefulness of her eccentric and exasperating family.

"Yeah, that's them. Terry with a *y* and Terri with an *i*." Jason Joe nodded, apparently pleased to have that settled. "Well, anyhoo, you know how relentless your mom is. She got everybody in the whole fam-dam-ly to start calling around. Your mom was the lucky one, though. She'd asked Terri to mark the most popular hotels on the list and she started off by calling those first. Three calls in, she asked for you at this place and what d'ya know? Here you were. So, here I am to take you back to Texas."

There was suddenly a death grip around her knees, and in a glance, Libby saw Sallie's apprehension. "Don't go, Libby," she pleaded. "Don't go to Tektheth. Don't go."

Alex didn't throw his arms around her legs, but his expression revealed a stark dismay. The same feeling clutched Libby like a fist to the stomach. She didn't want to go home. But Jason Joe showed no sign of letting go of her, either. And Ethan certainly wasn't making any protest. On the other hand, what was she waiting for—someone to step up and rescue her?

"Jason Joe," she said firmly, "there's something here you don't understand."

"You bet your boots, there is. When I got here, that guy over there—" he indicated the desk clerk with a nod "—wouldn't tell me your room number, wouldn't even tell me where you went, or when you left. Just says to me, real snootylike, 'You may wait, sir, if you wish.'" Jason Joe's chest swelled with resentment. "Well, you know that's as good as waving a red flag in front of Tat Owen's old bull. So I moseyed around, talking to people and asking if they'd seen you around. Turns out, you're here with some *other* man, some *loser* you picked up on the trip home." He sized Ethan up in an unimpressed glance. "An' I reckon this must be him."

"Yes," Libby confirmed, just as firmly, hoping she could stop Jason Joe from starting a fight he'd never win. Then, as her response registered, she quickly shook her head. "I mean, no, he isn't a loser and I didn't 'pick him up' on the trip home. It isn't anything like that. Ethan is my—"

"Fiancé." Ethan extended his hand in greeting. "I'm the man Libby went to Rome to marry, and I *reckon* that makes you the broken heart she left behind."

IT WAS A BAD IDEA. Ethan couldn't imagine how he'd ever thought of it, much less said it aloud.

But there it was. Spoken. Hovering in the lobby of the Plaza Hotel. Sitting like an uninvited elephant right in the middle of a conversation that was none of his business. Libby couldn't have looked more astounded if an elephant had just squeezed through the revolving doors, marched up and offered to give her a tour of the circus. Truth be told, Ethan figured he looked a little astounded himself.

On the other hand, Jason Joe didn't appear all that surprised. He seemed to take the idea at face value...and very obviously wanted to give that face a fast, hard punch to the nose. His gaze turned to Libby, patently disbelieving. "Who is this guy?" he asked. "'Cause I gotta tell ya, Libby Ann, there's a limit to how much I'm willin' to forgive and forget."

Libby's chin came up...which was a good thing, because Ethan wasn't going to let this guy—or anyone else, for that matter—talk to her like that. Jason Joe might be a good old boy from Beauregarde, Texas, but he had a lot to learn about good manners, and if Libby hadn't called him on it, Ethan would have.

"There's nothing for you to forgive, Jason Joe," Libby said. "So why don't you just go on back home where you belong?"

"Oh, right. Like home isn't where you belong, too." He cut a resentful gaze at Ethan. "Like you're gonna be happy living with some guy other than me."

"Were you *living* with him?" Ethan asked her, not at all happy with that possibility.

"Are you living with *him?*" Jason Joe wanted to know.

"No!" Libby looked from one man to the other. "No. I'm not living with either one of you."

"Not until after the wedding, anyway," Ethan added, God knew why. Except that his protective instincts were on full alert.

"What wedding?" Jason Joe strung a gaze from Ethan to Libby and back again. "You're not already married, are you?" His incredulous expression settled on Libby. "You didn't marry this yahoo in Rome, did you? I thought you went there to marry that Nick person, that Italian guy."

"Nick is a louse," Ethan said forcefully. "And I'm a lucky guy." Bad idea or not, he wasn't going to let this Mr. America wannabe waltz in here and whisk Libby back to Beauregarde without a fight. No one was going to do that to his kids. They needed Libby, for Pete's sake. Besides, she didn't want to go home. She'd said so.

"Libby wants to have the wedding at home with her family."

"No, she doesn't," Jason Joe argued. "Well, yes, she does. But not with you. She wants to marry me. She's just confused. You've got her all confused." He glanced at Libby. "You're confused."

"She's not confused," Ethan stated, trying to recall one single rule of successful negotiating, because he sure as hell had forgotten everything he knew about the subtle techniques of persuasion...and sanity. Something about this guy tripped his wire. Something about his blond, boy-next-door good looks had Ethan squaring off for a wrestling match. Something about the way Jason Joe looked at Libby, hugged her, held on to her, egged Ethan on to greater lunacy. "She said no when you asked her to marry you and she meant no. She said yes when I asked her and she meant yes. That doesn't sound confused to me."

"I've known Libby Ann all my life, and I'm tellin' you she's confused." He looked directly at her again. "You're confused, Libby, and I'm takin' you home right now."

"I'm not confused..." Libby began.

"Yes, you are, and you're probably going to stay that way until I get you out of this honky-tonk hotel.'' Jason Joe made an unsuccessful attempt to gather her hands into his.

Libby stepped out of his reach. ''I'm not going anywhere with you.''

''Yes, you are, because I sure as heck can't go back without you,'' Jason Joe stated, then dropped his give-me-a-hundred-pushups-and-nononsense tone of voice to a gentler, more persuasive pitch. ''I promised your mom I wouldn't come home unless you were with me. Come on, Libby, you know you don't really want to marry this old fart. Hell, I could see why some young, smooth-talkin', hand-kissin' Italian might turn your head, but this guy? He isn't even foreign.''

Old? Ethan blinked. Had this pigskin-headed galoot just called him *old?* ''I'll have you know I'm as Italian as ravioli.''

Libby and Jason Joe both turned to look at him, and Ethan felt like an idiot. What the hell was he arguing about? For all he knew, his ancestors had come from Dubuque, Iowa. But Jason Joe had no way of knowing that. Heck, Jason Joe wouldn't figure it out if Ethan claimed to be a direct descendant of the Pope. ''I,'' he continued coolly, ''am as Italian as macaroni.''

''You don't *look* Italian.'' Jason Joe didn't spend his afternoons coaching high school football players for nothing; he could call plays faster than any quarterback at fourth and goal. "You don't *sound* Italian." His gaze dropped to Sallie and Alex. "And they sure as shootin' aren't Italian."

That did it. Whatever good sense Ethan had left flew the coop at that point. He put a hand on each of his children's heads. "They are. I am. And Libby is gonna be. *Eye-towel-yun,* that is." He mimicked Jason Joe's pronunciation, his muscles tensed and ready for challenge, his chin leading the way. "You got a problem with that?"

Jason Joe's all-American chin lifted, his jaw squared. "Oh, yeah," he said. "I've got a real problem with that, Redwine. Hell, your name isn't even Italian. Sounds more Californicated to me."

Ethan clenched his jaw, telling himself not to sink to the level of this overgrown adolescent. On the other hand, he wasn't going to back down. Not over something as ethnic as his name. "It's Italian, all right. Used to be spelled with an *i* on the end, but immigration officials wrote it down as Redwine and that's what it's been ever since."

"Red-wi-ni?" Jason Joe repeated, finding his own pronunciation, as he seemed prone to do, then turning to Libby. "You want to go through life with a name like that?"

"No…" Libby began.

"Yes, she does," Ethan interrupted. "Because it's a good name, it's my name, and she likes it."

Jason Joe's shoulders went back, making him resemble a box. An icebox. Ethan squared his shoulders too, making the subtle point that no icebox should pick a quarrel with a refrigerator.

Subtlety was wasted on Jason Joe. "Why don't you just let Libby speak for herself? She wants to go home with me, and if you'll shut up for a minute, she'll tell you that." He kept his eyes narrowed on Ethan as he jerked his head toward Libby. "Tell him," he said.

"Tell *him*," Ethan said.

"No, tell *him*," Jason Joe repeated, apparently believing that, the louder the voice, the stronger the argument. "Tell him, Libby Anne."

Libby stood there, not telling either one of them anything, her big blue eyes shifting from one man to the other in mute and acute astonishment.

"Libby?" Sallie's voice quavered up from the vicinity of Libby's knees. "Am I goin' to Tektheth, too?"

"Right now," Libby said in a voice of steely softness, "you're going upstairs. I'm taking you and Alex upstairs. Just the three of us. You, me and Alex. Right now." And with a warning arch of her brows in Ethan's direction, she gathered both children between her hands and marched them toward the elevator bays.

Leaving in her wake, Ethan, Jason Joe and the aftermath of the very bad idea.

"ARE THERE VIDEO VILLAGE stores in Texas, Libby?" Alex asked in the elevator on the way up.

"Can I see the llamanaminal?" Sallie wanted to know.

"Llama," Libby corrected her absently...her thoughts in a whirling upheaval over what had just happened downstairs. The scene repeated over and over in her head, mainly the part where Ethan had inexplicably introduced himself as her fiancé. *Fiancé*, he'd said, *I'm her fiancé*. Unbelievable. Crazy.

And yet there was a loopy thrill that buzzed through her every time she thought about it. *Fiancé. I'm her fiancé.*

What had possessed him to utter those words? Jason Joe was obnoxious and stubborn as a one-eyed mule, but certainly no threat to Ethan. Had he thought Jason Joe meant to sling her over his shoulder and carry her back to Beauregarde?

Well, in all honesty, she'd thought that a distinct possibility, herself. But still... *Fiancé*.

Men had been falling all over themselves to protect her as long as she could recall. From the moment she started to walk, her brothers and cousins had been charged with the responsibility of "keeping an eye on Libby." She'd never climbed a tree without a helping hand, never been allowed to roughhouse with the boys, never even gone on a date when there wasn't a Waldron hovering somewhere close by. No dates until college, anyway...and she wasn't entirely sure that some member of the family hadn't been "keeping an eye on her" then, too. Not that she'd needed family to protect her when practically every male she met took one look at her and decided she was an innocent adrift in a dangerous world and that he— the man of the moment—would be her man-of-the-hour.

Except, Ethan hadn't treated her that way. He'd offered her fair exchanges right down the line— a plane ticket for taking care of his kids, room and board for her services as a temporary nanny, her conversation for his, his smiles for hers. He'd expected her to find her way around New York City with only a few cautionary instructions...and he'd entrusted his children to her charge while she did it, too. Not once had he stepped in to rescue her. Until now.

Fiancé, he'd said. *I'm her fiancé.*

The thrill made another unsettling loop across her heartstrings, despite the knowledge that her self-appointed *fiancé* had just unleashed a whole swarm of trouble.

THERE WASN'T ENOUGH to do in the lobby, Ethan discovered. Once you'd thoroughly explored the gift shops, had a cup of coffee in the Oak Room, a drink or two in the bar, chatted with the bell captain and watched people come and go for nearly an hour, the hotel lobby just didn't have much more to offer. With a heavy-duty frown, he decided he had no choice but to go upstairs to his room and face Libby.

He headed for the elevators with a whole pocketful of dread. Most of the time, he had really good ideas. Occasionally, he even had brilliant ones. But once in a great while, he had a flash of genuine insanity. And claiming to be Libby's fiancé had been a stroke of sheer, unmitigated lunacy.

Ethan punched the elevator button and waited, wishing Jason Joe had just punched him in the nose early on and put him out of his misery. Libby, he had a feeling, wouldn't be so kind.

"I'M SORRY," HE SAID the minute he'd closed the door behind him.

"Shh," Libby replied, holding up her hand to signal that he should hold his peace until she was off the phone. "No, I wasn't *shushing* you, Mom. Yes, of course, I'm listening."

"Daddy! Daddy!" Sallie bounced twice on the sofa, then hit the floor at a run to throw herself into Ethan's arms. "Daddy, gueth what?"

"What?" Ethan asked, his focus still on Libby, his not-overly-sensitive male antennae trying to pick up any indicators as to the degree of humiliation he was about to suffer. "What, Sallie?"

"I'm goin' to Tektheth!" She all but danced in his arms. "I'm gonna thee cowth and dogth an' kiddy catth an'...an' a bunch of llamanaminalth."

"Oh, that'll be nice." He absently set her on her feet and continued to stand awkwardly, hesitantly by the door. Quick getaways had never been his forte, but he might get lucky.

"Hey, Dad." Alex poked his head around the corner of the bedroom. "Do you think maybe I ought to get some boots before we go?"

"Boots?" Ethan repeated with a frown. "Snow boots?"

Alex grinned as if that were funny. "Libby already told me it doesn't snow in Texas."

Ethan began to get a glimmer of consequences. "I believe it, uh, does snow in the Panhandle."

"Oh, Dad," Alex said in preadolescent frustration. "We're not going to some pan place. We're going to *Texas* and I need some cowboy boots!" He closed the bedroom door, but not before Ethan heard his son's falsetto *"Oh, I'm a long, tall, Texan...!"*

Sallie hugged him around the knees. "I need cow bootth, Daddy! For when I see the llamanaminal." Then she danced away from him, singing "I'm a long, tall Tekthan, too."

And that was pretty much what Ethan had been afraid of...Texas. And it was his own damn fault. He looked at Libby, who was still listening, still holding the phone an inch from her ear, still looking like she'd rather be pinching someone's head. Most likely, his.

"Mom, would you let me get a word in—" Libby rolled her eyes toward the ceiling, then turned away from Ethan's gaze to look out the window while she listened, presumably, to her mother.

Okay, Ethan thought. The best thing to do was to... He couldn't think of a single *good* thing to do at the moment, must less the *best* thing. He could get Sallie out of the room, remove her cheerful little presence and give Libby some privacy. On the other hand, that could be interpreted as the coward's way out. Or in Texas, he supposed they'd called it a yellow-livered, yellow-bellied, yellow-dog coward's way out. Ethan ran a hand through his hair...something he rarely did...and contemplated the ripple effect of claiming to be Libby's fiancé in front of Jason Joe, the man who wanted to be her fiancé. Why hadn't he just let the muscle man sling her over his shoulder and carry her back to Texas? Now *that* would have been the easy way to resolve this. *That* would have been the best thing to do.

"Oh, I'm a long, tall Tekthan," Sallie sang, marching back and forth on the sofa cushions and belting out the song into one of Ethan's shoes, pretending it was a microphone. *"I ride a big, old llamanaminal!"*

"Mom," Libby said, then louder, "Mom? Mom, no, don't put Grampa on the phone. I need to talk to—hi, Grampa. How're you? Oh, I'm sorry to hear that." She paused and then raised her voice. "I said, I'm sorry to hear your arthritis has been acting up."

"Tha-boom-tha-boom-tha-boom." Sallie, the songstress, began a big finish that went on and on and...

The sick feeling in Ethan's stomach suddenly vanished, replaced with the warm, vibrant pleasure of discovery. Sallie was singing. His sad, silent little daughter was *singing*. And smiling. Dancing, too. And his introspective, introverted son wanted a pair of cowboy boots. Not a video game. A pair of cowboy boots. Ethan felt a smile begin...and just when he thought he'd never smile again.

Okay, so it had been wrong to claim he was going to marry Libby. If he'd thought about it for five seconds, he would have kept his mouth shut and let Libby handle her own problems, namely ex-boyfriend, Jason Joe. Ethan shouldn't have interfered, he knew that now. But he had interfered, and maybe he had done so because his subconscious was prompting him to hold on to Libby no matter what. She had worked a miracle with Alex and Sallie. Somehow she'd been able to touch their young and wounded hearts. Somehow she'd taught them to sing. Somehow she'd filled an empty space in their lives that the mother who'd abandoned them would never fill. Pretending to be Libby's fiancé was a bad idea. And he'd readily admit that a marriage for the sake of the kids was a perfectly awful idea. But if she'd agree, he'd marry her tomorrow, without a moment's hesitation. Sallie and Alex needed Libby. And because they did, Ethan would move heaven and earth to keep her.

"Dad," Libby said into the phone. "Hi. Yes, I'm fine. Really. Yes. Ye-e-s. I've been very careful and I always look both ways before I cross the street." She pulled the receiver a little farther from her ear. "No, I'm *not* being sassy with you. It's just that—" Her voice rose in both tone and tempo. "No, please, Dad. I'd rather just talk to you right now— *Hi,* Aunt Tina. How are you? Yes, Mom told me about that. I think lavender and green would be lovely together. Yes, yes, of course it is." Libby sighed. "Whatever you and Mom and Aunt Azalea decide will be fine. I trust your judgment." Another pause, another soft sigh. "Sure, put her on the other extension. The more, the merrier."

BY THE TIME SHE GOT OFF the phone, Libby felt like she'd been run over by a truck. A Mack truck. Something with the power of five hundred horses and tires as big as a flying saucer. All in all, a typical conversation with her family. She looked over at Ethan, who was holding Sallie on his lap while he read *The Poky Little Puppy*. His green eyes met hers, and a sliver of attraction cut through Libby's lassitude. Okay, so her family was nuts, so she hadn't been able to work an explanation into the conversation, so she hadn't done much in the way of damage control, and they mostly had the wrong impression about when, where and who she supposedly was marrying.

Truthfully, she was pretty confused about that herself. But watching Ethan read to his daughter, listening to the husky resonance of his voice, she felt fairly clear on where she wanted to be and who she wanted to be with…even if she hadn't a prayer of ever making her boisterous family understand.

Alex jerked open the bedroom door. "Libby? Do I need to take my coat?"

"A light jacket," she answered. "If you have one."

"Like a warm-up?"

"Yes, that'll be all the coat you need."

He smiled, as if the idea of not needing a coat

was better than a trip to Disneyland. "Cool," he said, and slammed the door.

"I needta pack," Sallie announced, wriggling off Ethan's lap and heading for the bedroom, the rest of the story forgotten for the moment.

"Don't touch anything in my suitcase, Sallie. I mean it." Alex's voice slipped through the ten-second crack between the opening and closing of the door, and then, without further ado, Libby was alone with her *fiancé*.

Chapter Seven

Libby looked out the window, taking a minute to compose her thoughts while she admired the view of Central Park. Then she took a deep breath and offered a tentative "Well, this has been an eventful afternoon."

Ethan pushed up from the chair and walked over to stand beside her. "I suppose I should offer you some sort of—"

"Explanation?" Libby suggested.

"I wish I had one to give. I was thinking more along the lines of an apology."

"Oh, right. Sorry. I should have let you finish your sentence." She wrinkled her nose. "Trying to carry on a conversation with members of my family brings out the worst in me. It may take a couple of stops and starts, but I'll do my best not to interrupt you again."

"Don't try too hard. Interruptions might make this easier."

She let a faint smile tip the corners of her mouth. "Believe me, the way my family does it, nothing gets easier."

"Sort of like my saying I was your fiancé when I should have kept my mouth shut?"

"You did rather complicate my life at that point."

He shoved his hands into the pockets of his slacks. "I am sorry, Libby. I don't know what possessed me to say such a thing…unless it was the way he talked to you. Every time he opened his mouth, I had this mental image of him patting you on the head like you were a prize beagle."

She laughed. "With Jason Joe, I'd have to be a bird dog to get any real pats on the head. He can be…difficult."

"Yes, well, I have no excuse for the way I behaved, and I do, most humbly, apologize. You must have thought I'd lost my mind."

"I was pretty surprised." She turned her head toward the view of Central Park, because with Ethan so close to her she found it hard to catch her breath. "Not quite as surprised as Jason Joe, but…" She risked another glance at Ethan and

felt, again, a scintillating ripple of awareness.
"By the way, what did you do with him?"

Ethan grinned. "You make it sound like I put
him in a pair of concrete galoshes and tossed him
into the East River."

"I guess he wasn't quite *that* obnoxious. I was
afraid there might have been a, uh, loud exchange
of words."

"No. After you left he didn't seem much inclined to exchange anything except dirty looks.
When I got tired of making faces at him, I asked
if he wanted to have a cup of coffee with me, but
he said he wasn't interested in furthering our acquaintance."

"He said that?" Libby doubted Jason Joe had
ever used that expression in his life.

"Maybe not those *exact* words, but I'm pretty
sure it's what he meant."

"Mmm," Libby said, appreciating the fact that
Ethan wasn't going to give her all the gory details.
"But he did finally leave?"

"He did."

"Peacefully?"

Ethan cleared his throat. "For the most part.
He wasn't completely sold on the idea of leaving
the hotel until he tried to get a room for the night.
A brief conversation with the front desk clerk

seemed to change his mind rather abruptly, though. He said something to me about the Big Apple costing more than a pickup load of cow manure—although those weren't his *exact* words, either.''

''Diplomacy has never been his strong suit.''

''Really?'' Ethan said with a quiet smile. ''I never would have guessed.''

''So, do you think he was going on home without me?''

Ethan's zeroed in on her hopeful tone. ''I only just met the man, but my guess is he'd rather spend the rest of his life in this rotten apple of a city than go home without you in tow. I suppose there's always a chance he'll leave on his own. He didn't actually say where he was going. Then again, we weren't on the best of terms when he departed.''

She sighed. ''You're right. He won't give up so easily. Frankly, I'm surprised he came all the way to New York City to get me, although my family must have put him up to it. They've made no secret of the fact that they'd love to see me married to him.'' Libby pushed a wayward strand of hair away from her face, tucking the ends behind her ear. ''They probably convinced him I'd be *thrilled* to have him *fetch* me home. Although

I really shouldn't complain. If it had been someone else waiting for us in the lobby…'' She let
the sentence trail off, guessing that if Jason Joe
hadn't been the one sent to *fetch* her, if it had
been her father or one of her brothers, she'd be
on her way home at this very moment, regardless
of her personal feelings on the matter. She cut her
gaze to Ethan, knowing her reprieve was probably
going to be short-lived. ''You should be grateful
for that small providence, too. My brothers have
even less diplomacy than Jason Joe.''

''Thanks for the warning. I'll try to be better
prepared next time.'' Ethan stroked a hand along
his jaw. ''I'm just sorry I acted like such a fool.
Jumping in to rescue you when you, obviously,
could have handled Jason Joe with more aplomb
than I did.''

She gave a short, soft laugh. ''I don't know
about *aplomb,* but I don't think I could have done
any worse. Now he thinks I'm going to marry
you.''

''It isn't quite as bad as you make it sound,
Libby. It'll just require a little explaining, that's
all.''

A little explaining. Right. She sighed, long and
deeply. ''What am I going to do, Ethan? My family is in the throes of wedding preparations, as it

is. They think I'm coming home tomorrow with Jason Joe and they've planned parties and barbecues and Lord only knows what else to celebrate.''

"I suppose you didn't get much of an opportunity to set the record straight when you were talking to them on the phone just now?''

The wayward strand of hair escaped, and she tucked it behind her ear again. ''They didn't give me much of a chance, but then I'm not sure I know how to set the record straight on this one, anyway. I told them over and over again that I wasn't going to marry Jason Joe, but until I got on the plane to Rome, they thought I was being coy. Returning to Beauregarde without the husband I told them I was bringing isn't going to help my credibility.'' The complications seemed endless now, the explanation too tangled to ever unravel. ''One minute I tell myself I should buck up, go back and face the music. But the next minute, I'm positive the only music I'd be facing is the wedding march.''

"They can't make you marry him, can they?''

"No. At least, I don't think so. But sometimes, they're so *set* on a plan that everything, and everybody, just seems to fall in line. And in the past, that's included me. They have this way of making something you absolutely don't want to do seem like the right thing to do.''

"I'll go with you," Ethan said quietly. "Sallie, Alex and I will go with you, and together we'll think of some way to put things right.''

A little knot of anxiety vied with a ready pleasure at his offer. If Ethan was with her, Libby was sure she could handle the chaos of miscommunication that was a Waldron family habit. He would give her someone sane to talk to. He could even *be* her fiancé for a few days, just until the hoopla settled down and she could figure out how to explain why she'd only thought she wanted to marry Nick Carlucci, and why she still didn't want to marry Jason Joe Johnson, and why she was only pretending she wanted to marry Ethan Redwine. He could be her buffer between the forcefulness of her family's desire to see her marry Jason Joe and her own steadfast refusal to settle for less than she deserved. It could work. It could. Except for one thing.

"But how can we put Alex and Sallie through that?" she asked. "What are they going to think?"

"That Texas is a great place to visit?"

"You know what I mean, Ethan. They're young, but they're not dumb. They'd get caught up in my family's enthusiasm over a wedding and wind up being hurt when they find out it was just a big pretense.''

He was quiet for a long time, until Libby almost believed his attention had drifted to other things, more solvable problems. But then he stepped closer to the window, closer to her, and softly said, ''What if it wasn't a pretense? What if we go to Beauregarde together and go through with the ceremony? Let your family and friends set your feet on the path to wedded bliss with me?''

Her throat went tight, and the elusive thrill of excitement whipped like a high-speed roller coaster around her heart. ''It wouldn't be bliss, though, would it, Ethan? It would be just plain nutty.''

''You think so?''

''Well, of course. Don't you? We haven't even known each other a whole week.''

''It doesn't take long to know the important things, Libby.''

''Maybe not, but it takes time to learn to love another person and we're...well, we're certainly not in love with each other.''

He turned to look at her, and something in the

depths of his eyes gave her pause. He couldn't *possibly* be serious. Could he?

"But that's the appeal of it, Libby," he said, sounding dead serious. "I'm not going to fall victim to some crazy and mistaken idea of love ever again, and you said yourself that you were through with romance. When you stop to think about it, my off-the-wall remark about being your fiancé may have real merit. In one step, you'd be free of Jason Joe and the well-meaning interference of family and friends."

"Marrying you to keep from marrying him seems a bit drastic," she said over the tumultuous rhythm of her heartbeat. It was a crazy idea. She could hardly believe Ethan had even thought of it, much less said it aloud. So why was her whole body tensed and eager to discuss the possibility? Why couldn't she just laugh…as he was probably expecting her to do…and let the whole thing blow over? "We barely know each other."

His expression changed, became wry and regretful. "You're right. It doesn't make any sense. I guess I thought…well, you seemed so acquiescent the minute Jason Joe appeared on the scene, so ready to knuckle under to his assertion that he knew what was best for you. I don't want you to get home and find yourself unable to stand up to

the combined pressures of him and your family.''
He paused, shrugged. ''But it was crazy of me to
have even said it out loud.'' His smile curved
slowly and was startlingly attractive. ''I'm probably just being selfish, anyway. I had hoped I
could persuade you to stay on with the kids and
me, help us get settled in a house, teach me how
to relate to Alex and Sallie the way you do. But
it's a bad idea. Forget it.''

''No,'' she said quickly, impulsively. ''I'd like
to stay on with you and the kids, Ethan. Really.
But, well, marriage is...so, so permanent.''

''Permanent?'' He looked away from her for
the first time since this strange conversation had
begun. ''Diane certainly didn't consider it permanent, and I stopped thinking about it in terms
of happily-ever-after a long time ago. Dealing
with contracts all the time, I tend to view most
everything as some form of negotiation. Once you
remove the romantic nonsense and starry-eyed illusions, marriage is basically a nonbinding contract negotiated between two consenting adults.''
He turned his gaze to her again and lifted his
shoulder in an offhand shrug. ''But I have no
business pushing my cynical views on you, Libby.
You're absolutely right. It's a bad...a *very* bad
idea.''

"I didn't say it was a *bad* idea." It was, but he'd been incredibly kind to her and she couldn't think of any job she'd rather have than taking care of Alex and Sallie. And Ethan, too. Except, of course, he didn't need any taking care of. "I'm flattered you thought of it," she continued. "But marriage is more than signing a contract. I mean, there are some things that just aren't, well, negotiable."

"Really? Like what?"

Libby frowned, wishing she was as quick with answers as he was with questions. "Well, like…like breakfast."

"You don't think breakfast is negotiable?"

"Not if you like bacon and eggs at seven o'clock at the kitchen table and your spouse prefers cinnamon and sugar doughnuts at eleven while watching television in the den."

He laughed, a wonderful, husky chuckle. "Negotiable. Three days a week we eat bacon and eggs at seven, three days we have doughnuts at eleven, leaving one day for spontaneity…or pancakes."

"What if I—I mean, the *spouse* is, oh…say…a vegetarian?"

"We switch to bagels and cream cheese or we eat at the Good Earth deli around the corner." He spread his hands in a congenial gesture. "See? Breakfast is negotiable."

"What about toothpaste?" Her parents were always arguing about toothpaste. "What if you like minty-fresh gel and I...I mean, your *spouse* likes original flavor paste? What if she squeezes from the middle and you roll from the bottom?"

"Two tubes," he said with a shrug, and Libby wondered why that hadn't occurred to her...or her mom and dad. "It's compromise, Libby, and compromise is the cornerstone of negotiations...and marriages."

It sounded reasonable. Even realistic. But she couldn't believe marriage was basically so simple. Not when there was emotion involved. And kids. And sex. Sex always complicated a relationship. "But there's more to it than that, Ethan. There are, uh, other shared elements, you know."

There was the slightest twitch at one corner of his mouth, a flash of humor in his green eyes. "Shared elements," he repeated. "Something more complex than bacon and bagels, more complicated than toothpaste. Like what, Libby? Where to live? What school the kids should attend? How to divide up any disposable income? All negotiable points, I assure you."

She felt a soft, self-conscious blush invade her

cheeks, wanted to cover them with her palms, so he wouldn't know how far her imagination had flown from bacon and eggs and toothpaste tubes. But she knew, even as she tucked the errant strand of hair behind her ear again, that cover-up was impossible. He could probably tell by looking at her that sex was on her mind. "Well," she said bravely. "Married people generally share a...a bed."

"A king-size if you like lots of room, a queen-size if you like to snuggle." He stroked his chin, as if considering the problem. "Of course, the size of the bed isn't really the compromise here. There'd have to be some agreement on how much distance constitutes lots of room and how often there would be snuggling. Also, how much snuggling is satisfactory." He nodded, thoughtfully. "I can see where this part of the negotiation could get a little...sticky."

"I wasn't talking about the bed itself," she said, feeling the soft warmth of embarrassment turn heated and rosy beneath her skin. "I was talking about...well, about things that might happen in it...other than snuggling, that is. Or sleeping."

"Oh..." He raised his eyebrows. "You meant...that *other* element." Again he stroked his jaw, as if the subject was perplexing. "You meant..." He lowered his voice to a hushed but seductive whisper. *"Sex."*

Why had she ever started this? Libby wondered, but she wasn't going to let him see how embarrassed she really was. "Yes," she said. "I'm afraid that sex just isn't negotiable."

He frowned. "Oh, I see. I guess you're right about that. If you don't find me sexually attractive, then there's not much I can do to change your mind."

"I didn't say that," Libby blurted out, too quickly, too forcefully, too...everything to explain it away with any grace. "I didn't say you weren't...that I didn't find you.... Well, I mean, you're obviously not unattractive, and maybe under the right circumstances, we might discover..." Oh, man, she was never going to get her tongue out of this tangle. "Would you just forget I said that?" she requested softly. "Just...just forget it, okay?"

"No, I don't think so, Libby." His voice was as smooth as the seamless movement of his hands to her shoulders. "You've brought up a very good point. Sexual compatibility. I don't think that could be a negotiable point. It's either there...or it isn't. And that, conceivably, could be a deal breaker. What do you think?''

Think? He expected her to *think* when the warmth of him was flowing through his palms, across her shoulders, along her arms, shivering down her back in a flood tide of awareness.

''Think we ought to find out now...before this negotiation goes any further?''

Oh, yes, she definitely thought they should. Although, she couldn't exactly remember what they were negotiating. Not that it mattered when he pulled her toward him by slow degrees, promising a world of sweet compromises, offering an exchange of enticing desires, giving her plenty of opportunities to withdraw gracefully.

Libby rejected every objection her conscience whipped out and went eagerly, if slowly, into his arms, ready and willing to participate in this experiment when, on one level, she knew she ought to refuse. But the reasons she ought to refuse eluded her.

Ethan's hands were strong and possessive on her shoulders, and their warmth remained even as his palms lifted to cup her face with the same possessive assurance. His gaze held steady on hers, keeping her a willing participant, until the moment he bent his head and her eyelids drifted closed. Somewhere in the vicinity of her heart, she began to tremble and her lips took the cue. She breathed in the faint, familiar scents of coffee, Scotch and October, and then his mouth was on hers and her head was beating, her heart spinning.

Er, no, it was her head that was spinning, her heart that was beating. Pounding, really. Nothing made sense and nothing else mattered. Except his lips, moving against hers in small, scintillating circles, luring her deeper into his kiss, making her aware that of all the men who had kissed her at one time or another, Ethan was the only one who had the faintest idea of how it ought to be done. Boy, did he have a good idea. She'd never been kissed so...thoroughly. Or tenderly. Or with such flare. In school, chemistry had never held much interest for her, but now she realized she simply hadn't understood how it worked. Until Ethan's kiss, until every nerve in her body began shorting out in response. Somewhere, on the fringes of her consciousness, Libby remembered this kiss was experimental. What kind of experiment, though, eluded her. Something about compromises. Or toothpaste. Or having bacon on a bagel. She couldn't remember. But whatever it was he'd set out to prove, she was willing to christen it a rousing success.

"Dad?" Alex's voice was close. Very close. Reluctantly, with a lingering nibble, Ethan drew back from the kiss, leaving Libby weak-kneed but still standing...barely. "Yes, Alex?" Ethan's voice was husky and thick, and the trembling inside of Libby began all over again at the raw sound of it. "Something you need, son?"

Alex looked from one adult to the other, and then a wide, hopeful grin split his expression. "Are you and Libby gonna get married? Is that why we're going to Texas? Is it?"

"We're going to Texas so you can have an excuse to wear cowboy boots and so Sallie can pet a llama."

"And a horthe, Daddy," said Sallie, suddenly appearing at the door. Giving Libby a hearty hug at the knees, she added, "An' a cow. An' a bunch of other aminaminalth."

"So, are you?" Alex asked again. "Are you getting married?"

Ethan's arm went around Libby's shoulders. "We're thinking about it."

Libby frowned up at him, her thoughts neither clear nor connected, her lips still recovering from his kiss. "Thinking," she repeated thickly. "We're thinking?"

Ethan's hand squeezed her upper arm reassuringly. "That's right," he said. "Just thinking."

But something in the look he gave her, something settled and confident in the curve of his lips…the lips that had just kissed her senseless…made Libby think it was a done deal. Made her wonder how, in the space of one mindboggling kiss, she had leaped from Jason Joe's frying pan into a fire hot enough to seriously singe her heart.

AS SHE CLOSED THE BACK book flap of *The Poky Little Puppy,* Libby wondered if it had occurred yet to Ethan that he'd asked her to marry him. Well, not actually *asked,* maybe, but the offer was on the table nonetheless. She still thought he'd just made a mistake, had a little glitch in his brain waves that was bound to correct itself sooner or later. At any moment, she expected to hear him say a profound "Oops!"

She pulled the coverlet up from the foot of the bed to cover Sallie and resolutely refused to look across to where Ethan was doing the same for Alex. The whole tucking-in ritual seemed fraught with intimacy and hidden meaning…even though it was the same ritual they'd performed every night since they'd arrived in New York. Ethan wasn't behaving like a man who'd just made a completely outlandish proposal. It was only Libby whose heart still seemed to be spinning from the afternoon's events, from that mind-altering kiss. Only Libby who wasn't sure whether she ought to believe Jason Joe, who'd told her she was confused, or Ethan, who'd assured her she was not.

On the one hand, Jason Joe was a hothead. And on the other hand, Ethan wasn't. He was level-headed. Sane. Sensible. But that didn't do anything to explain how, in the blink of an eye, she'd gone from being a hired nanny to Ethan's children to being his prospective bride.

Bride. The very word sent a shiver down her spine. It wasn't the same shiver she'd felt when Jason Joe proposed. It wasn't the same shiver she'd felt when she'd walked into Nick's bedroom at his villa and realized she didn't want to marry him, either. Oh, no, this shiver felt a lot like the one she'd experienced the moment Ethan had asked her to switch seats on the plane and sit next to him. A lot like the shiver that continued to attack her at random moments when Ethan looked at her, or spoke to her, or moved, or walked or breathed. And now that he'd kissed her, that same shiver trickled down her spine every single time she thought about kissing him again...and she could hardly think of anything else. Her lips were still warm with the memory, her knees still felt like they were filled with Jell-O. Lemon Jell-O, the color of cowardice and weak knees.

Maybe she should start laughing and tell Ethan she'd just now gotten the punch line. Turn the whole thing into a dumb-blonde joke. But the idea of him laughing, too, wasn't funny. None of her options offered much in the way of amusement. Facing Jason Joe again wouldn't be a barrel of laughs, and facing her family...well, that was about the least funny thing Libby could imagine at the moment.

What was funny, was she kept thinking that being engaged to Ethan wasn't a bad idea at all. Her imagination kept drifting into romantic scenarios of sharing his life, his children...his bed. In fact, marrying him was the single most appealing idea she'd had in years. It felt right and good, like the obvious answer to a perplexing question. Even if "romantic nonsense" was written all over it.

"Libby?" Sallie asked around a yawn that was nearly as big as she was. "I wanna hear about your dogth."

"Again?" Libby pulled the sheet up around Sallie's neck. "Aren't you tired of dog stories?"

Sallie shook her head, fanning her black hair across the white pillow in long strands of static cling. "I *love* them. I wanna hear the Panda thtory."

Libby smoothed the thick bangs across Sallie's forehead. It wasn't much of a story, but if Sallie liked it, at least it meant another few minutes before Libby had to be alone with Ethan and had to make either a joke or a decision. "I have three dogs," she began. "One big dog named Paw, one medium-size dog named Panda, and one little dog named Max. Paw is the youngest and Max is the oldest, and Panda is the one I rescued from mean old Jimmy Dan Dawson, who was trying to make the poor little thing jump through a ring of fire for his stupid make-believe circus."

"I've never been to the thircuth," Sallie said. "Did Panda like it?"

"Not when she knew she'd burn her paws if she tried to jump through the ring of fire."

"Ith Panda thmart, Libby?"

Libby nodded, her thoughts a long way from her canine pets, focused instead on the man who had come to stand across from her, on the other side of Sallie's bed. His gaze rested on her for a moment and the shiver jogged in place.

"Libby has very smart dogs," Ethan said, pulling the covers up around his daughter's chin. "And tomorrow you'll meet all three of them. But tonight, Sallie, it's time for you to go to sleep."

"I wanna hear 'bout Panda." Sallie drew out the complaint, punctuating it with a yawn. "Libby wantth to tell me again."

"She's told that same story three times in the past thirty minutes and that's enough. Besides, you're keeping Alex awake with all the talking. Look at him. He's practically falling asleep over his video game."

Alex didn't even glance up, or yawn. "They're not keepin' me awake," he informed his father. "I like dog stories."

"You like anything that gives you a few more minutes with that silly game. Put it away, Alex, and go to sleep."

"But Dad, Libby showed me and Travis how to get the special key that opens the door of the dragon's lair, and I want to do it before he does."

"You can work at it on the plane tomorrow."

Libby stopped smoothing the comforter. In the corner, Alex's and Sallie's suitcases stood, packed and ready. *Texas, here we come.*

She didn't yet know how she could go to Texas, taking Alex and Sallie and Ethan, without explaining to someone that she wasn't really engaged, wasn't really planning to marry anyone, wasn't really sure she knew what had happened to her last engagement or how her current false engagement had come into being. But she did know that if she didn't go home—with or without Ethan—there'd be reinforcements on the way to New York City by this time tomorrow. And she definitely did not want to face any Waldrons in the lobby of the Plaza Hotel.

"Good night." She bent to kiss Sallie's cheek. As she lifted her head, Ethan bent to kiss Sallie, too, and his hand came to rest over Libby's on the turned-down edge of the sheet. Libby couldn't have moved away from that touch if, at that very minute, Panda had needed to be rescued from mean old Jimmy Dan Dawson.

"Good night, princess," Ethan said to his daughter. "Sleep tight and dream of horses and llamas, okay?"

Her smile was little-girl sweet and sleepy. "Okay, Daddy. I'll dream about Panda an' Makth an' Paw an' cowth and all the other aminaminalth."

Ethan's gaze lifted to meet Libby's, sharing in

a look the simple joy of a child's good-night. Then his fingertip trailed across the back of her hand in a gliding promise before he turned to the other bed and deftly removed the video game from Alex's hot little hands. "Enough already, Alex. You can find the key another day. It'll still be there, I assure you."

"But, Dad..."

"Good night, Alex." He kissed him, too, and waited while Libby gave the covers one last tuck and Alex one last good-night kiss. Then Ethan took Libby's hand and led her from the room, switching off the light and pulling the door nearly closed behind them, leaving just enough opening for a wedge of light and security to shine through. Then, urgently, but without hurry, he drew Libby away from the doorway, pulled her into his arms and kissed her, too.

Only it wasn't a good-night kiss.

Unless she'd been wrong all these years about exactly what constituted a *good* night.

This time when he pulled back, keeping one hand braced against the wall, one hand curved around her waist, Libby noticed that he was none too steady, either. And she was pretty sure his breathing was as shallow as her own. And she thought it was his heartbeat she felt beneath her palm, pulsing hard and fast...although it could've been just the resonance of her own.

"Wow," he whispered, echoing her own battered and breathless awe. "I had to make sure I hadn't imagined how good that was."

Looking into his eyes, Libby knew she was going down, hook, line and mooring. This was not supposed to happen. Not like this. Not this fast. Not with this sudden rush of wanting. Not after she'd chased her own starry-eyed hopes to Rome and lost her foolish illusions of love and romance. Not when she couldn't think, couldn't see straight, couldn't even seem to stand under her own power.

His lips captured hers again, tasting her with tender, tantalizing nips and slow strokes of his tongue. Libby leaned into the kiss, feeling—yes— the excitement of his racing heart and the ragged edge of his breathing and the surprise that coursed between them, sensual and scary. It took some willpower, but she managed to push against his chest and gain some crucial space before the question of no-room-left-for-caution could arise. "Ethan," she said.

"Libby," he replied.

And for a long moment—a very long moment—that seemed to be enough. Except she had to leave. Libby knew it was now or never, and, with a gulp, she ducked under his arm and moved backward in the general direction of the front door, half afraid he'd come after her, half afraid he wouldn't.

Ethan kept his hand braced against the wall, his head resting on his upper arm, but before Libby could make good her escape, he straightened, looked her way, and then moved to intercept her. "Don't go," he said persuasively. "We should... talk."

Nodding, Libby managed to reach the door, open it—despite several fumbling attempts to turn the knob—and back into the hallway. She gripped the doorknob and held up a restraining hand to keep Ethan—and any further experimental kisses—at bay. Although she knew that if he came even another step closer, her restraint would desert her like a kite without a string. "We'll talk," she whispered hoarsely, wanting nothing more than to throw herself across the door sill and back into his arms. "Later."

"Tomorrow," he said, in the most seductive voice she'd ever heard. "We're going to Texas. I've never been to Texas, you know."

She hadn't known. Wasn't sure she knew now. Of course, who could think when his lips were

moving, when her imagination was consorting
with all kinds of fantasies, when in two steps she
could be in his arms and kissing him again. "Me,
neither," she whispered, oblivious to the words
she said, unaware if they were truth or lies.

"We'll go together, then."

She nodded, knowing she'd gotten lost, somehow, in his gaze. "I have to go to bed."

"Stay," he suggested. "Share mine."

There it was. Temptation. The siren's song.
And here she was without her earplugs. "Good
night, Ethan," she said, in the firmest tone she
could elicit from her tight throat. "Good night."

"Sweet dreams, Libby."

"Sweet dreams, Libby," she repeated, mesmerized by the movement of his mouth.

"I believe that's my line." He smiled...and her
heart urged her to stop hesitating in the doorway
and go back inside.

But she retained a glimmer of sanity. She had
to stop, think, get a good night's sleep and clear
her head before she did something more foolish
than flying off to Rome to marry a man who
thought four plus one made a pair. Grampa
George always said, *When confused...snooze,* and
that sounded like as good advice as she was apt
to get tonight. She took another step back, pro-

pelling her unwilling body from the doorway into the hall. "I'm leaving now."

"I could walk you to your door." He took a step toward her. "I wouldn't mind."

"I wouldn't mind, either," she said in a breathless rush of words. "That's why you have to stay here." Quickly, then, she jerked the door closed, leaving him on one side and her on the other. She didn't release the breath she'd been holding until she heard the audible click of the latch. Now, at least, she was safely in the hall and Ethan was safely *not*.

"I was beginning to think you weren't plannin' on sleepin' in your own bed tonight." The voice behind her was familiar, too close, and too confident for comfort.

She closed her eyes for a second, wishing she could have been somewhere else, anywhere else, right now. "Where I plan on sleeping is none of your business, Jason Joe. What are you doing out here in the hall, anyway? You nearly scared me to death."

"I've been waitin' for you, Libby Ann. Seems like I've been waitin' for you most of my life, and where you sleep is, too, my business. Seein' as how you're going to be my wife."

She sighed, not wanting to go over the same

old argument again. "Go home, Jason. You shouldn't have come here in the first place."

"Is that a fact?" His face was flushed with either excitement, liquor or both. His expression was linebacker determined. His stance, winner-take-all. "I've come a long way to rescue you, Libby Ann," he said evenly, firmly, thickly. "And I'm not leavin' here without you."

"You'll have to because I am not—repeat, I *am not*—going back to Beauregarde with you."

"Yeah, yeah, you've said stuff like that before, Miss Thinks-She-Needs-to-Be-Independent." The distance between them dissolved under his short, quick strides. "And I'm real sorry you feel that way, but you're goin' with me because it's what your folks want, it's what I want, and whether you believe it or not, it's what you want, too. Believe me, Libby Ann, this is for your own good."

He picked her up under one arm as easily as if she'd been a football he meant to carry across the goal line.

"Stop this!" She slapped his calf with her hand and kicked the air. "Put me down, Jason. Right now!" They were halfway to the elevator before she realized he wasn't going to stop or put her down. Jason Joe meant to take her home by hook, by crook or by quarterback carry.

She twisted her head to look up at him and gave him as serious a frown as was possible while bouncing like a rag doll under his arm. "Put me down, Jason, or I swear on our high school yearbook that I will tell everyone in town the real reason you fumbled the football in the last thirty seconds of the state championship game our senior year."

He caught her a little more firmly around the middle and kept walking. "You won't do that. Not to your husband-to-be."

"They'll take your trophy out of the Rebels' Hall of Fame."

He stopped but kept her tucked under his arm. "Gol darn it, Libby Ann, don't you want to go home?"

"No, she doesn't," Ethan said, his voice powerfully certain and deep behind them. "How many times does she have to tell you?"

Jason tossed a growl over his shoulder. "You stay out of this, city slicker. Libby's *my* fiancée and she's goin' with me. You got nothin' to say about it. And that's that."

"I believe I have something to say about it," Libby began, but her voice was no match for the escalating challenge between the two men.

"You're mistaken, cowboy." Ethan's tone

took up Jason's dare. "I believe you'll agree with me that a *husband* has plenty to say about where his wife goes and who she goes with."

Libby got a bad feeling about where this was headed, but at least she was no longer headed for the elevator. Or a touchdown.

"You betcha, I agree." Jason Joe hiked her higher under his arm and set off down the hall again, tossing his reason over his shoulder like a careless pinch of salt. "And since I'm the one who's gonna be her husband, I say she's goin' with me."

"Well, considering that I *am* her husband, I say she's not."

"Husband?" Libby whispered, while her heart did a free fall.

"Husband?" Jason Joe stiffened and stopped dead in his tracks. *"Husband?"* he repeated in a voice crisp with suspicion. "Just what in hell is he tryin' to tell me, Libby Ann?"

"Nothing," she said, hoping, praying, she'd misheard the whole thing.

"I'm telling you," Ethan continued, as if there could be no doubt, "that Libby isn't my fiancée. She's my *wife*."

"Wife?" Jason Joe sounded as stunned as if he had, impossibly, just scored a goal for the opposing team. "Did you just call my girlfriend your *wife?*"

Wife. Libby tried to twist free, but for all her wiggling, she barely caught a glimpse of Ethan, standing with feet apart, hands fisted at his sides. Obviously, that last kiss had affected her hearing or his memory, because he couldn't have...surely wouldn't have said—

"Wife." With the force of a bowling ball thundering down the hotel hallway, Ethan repeated the word in a steady, don't-mess-with-me voice, as if he'd said it a hundred times, as if it were a statement of fact, and therefore, inarguable. "*Wife* is what I said, and *wife* is what I meant. Now, kindly, let go of Libby, *my* wife."

Chapter Eight

For once in his life, Jason Joe Johnson did as he was told…and let go of Libby, dropping her like a bulky bag of potatoes as he spun to face Ethan, the challenger. Libby was unprepared for the sudden fall and caught her weight full on her right hand and knee. A sharp pain ricocheted all the way up her arm, but she kept her focus on the two men, especially the nearest one, the one who was squaring off to deliver a roundhouse punch in defense of her honor. Or dishonor. Or her marital status. Good grief, she thought, and scrambled to her feet. "Jason," she said firmly. "Stop it now. You are not going to start some vulgar brawl in this hallway."

"Fine," he said through clenched teeth. "We'll start it inside the room."

He took a menacing step toward Ethan, and

Libby grabbed his arm, feeling the pinch of pain again in her wrist. "You're not starting anything except a trip back to Texas."

Jason looked down at her. "What's the matter, Libby Ann? Isn't your *husband* man enough to fight for himself? Do you have to step in to protect the lily-livered jackrabbit?"

"I'm trying to protect you, you idiot." She squeezed his arm and winced with the effort.

"Are you all right, Libby?" Ethan asked.

"I'm fine," she answered, and renewed her attempt to keep the man who said he wanted to marry her from punching the man who claimed he *had* married her. "This is embarrassing enough without starting a stupid fistfight, Jason Joe. Go home. Now. Before I get really mad."

"You just go right on and get mad, Libby Ann, 'cause come hell or high water, I'm not going home without you. I don't care how many men say they're married to you. I know you weren't married when I proposed to you, and you didn't get married in Rome, and you're not married now. So, you know what that means?"

"I can still become a nun?"

"You're not even Catholic. What it means is that you're marryin' me next Saturday at the First

Methodist Church in Beauregarde, Texas.'' He scowled at Ethan. ''And he's not invited.''

''It's bad manners to exclude the husband.'' Ethan appeared completely calm, cool and collected. Not threatening or threatened. Not even a little agitated. ''But since Libby won't be there, either, we'll let etiquette slide this time.''

Jason Joe tensed anew. ''You are not her husband,'' he stated confidently. ''Earlier today, downstairs in the lobby, you said you were her fiancé. Well, that was a lie and this is a bigger one. Only difference is this time she's not rushing in to back you up. She hasn't once claimed she was married to *you*. So, back off, Redweenie. Libby Ann is my girl and she's goin' home with me.'' He reached for Libby's hands as if possession of them would prove his point and preclude any further argument. ''Tell him, Libby Ann. Tell him you're going to marry me.''

As his fingers closed over her hand and he tugged her to his side, a fire began in her wrist and burned its way all the way up her shoulder. She tried to keep her mind on Jason and Ethan and keeping the peace and stopping a brawl in the nicest hotel she'd ever stayed in, but her best intentions got lost in a wave of pain.

''Tell him,'' Jason commanded again. ''Tell

this big-city yahoo you're going to marry a real man. Tell him you're going to marry me.''

Libby could barely think past the escalating and distracting discomfort in her arm, barely keep her knees from buckling beneath her. "I can't tell him that," she said thickly, taking the path of least resistance. "He's my husband."

Then she fainted.

THROUGH A FOG of discomfort, Libby was aware of sharp words mixed with softer ones, a gentle probing along her arm, ice, heat, and the sting of a million needles. She was conscious throughout the flurry of activity around her, knew that she participated in the decision to go to the hospital, actively answered a multitude of questions about her injury, her allergies, and her insurance, and personally asked at least three times if Alex and Sallie were okay. It was Ethan's voice, too, that held the most comfort, the most concern, the most calm. But it was Jason Joe's contentious tones that brought her to a full and vexing wakefulness.

"She's *my* fiancée, and I'm not leaving her, no matter how many times you claim to be her husband!"

"Haven't you done enough damage to Libby without getting us all kicked out of the hospital?"

"I didn't *mean* to drop her and I sure as hell didn't want to hurt her, but there's something real fishy about this and I'm not leaving her until I know what it is."

Libby looked at the dark-haired nurse who was wrapping her wrist in a neon pink cast and listening with obvious fascination to the hoarsely whispered conversation of the two men. She probably didn't get too many patients with a broken wrist, a husband, and a fiancé, Libby thought with more generosity than she felt. Truth was, her arm throbbed, her shoulder ached, and the last thing she wanted to do was convince anyone she was married. "I'm married, Jason Joe," she said anyway, giving the lie as much definition as she could manage. "So would you please stop insisting I'm not and just...go away."

He looked down at her, all good-hearted and as stubborn as forty mules. "I'm not leaving your side, Libby," he said, reaching across the brunette to pat Libby's fair head. "I'll wait until you feel better before I take you home, so just don't you worry."

"I'm fine, really. You go on home, Jason Joe," she assured him.

He shook his head and smiled soothingly. "I've already phoned your folks and told 'em that nothing could pry me away from you until you're well enough to travel. Your mom wanted to come right on up here to take care of you, but I convinced her you were in good hands with me." He flashed a defiant look at Ethan, who stood, lips pursed, on Libby's other side. "I told her you were my fiancée and that meant, you were already in the best possible hands."

Libby had had similar conversations with Jason Joe and knew he wasn't going to budge in his convictions, but she still lifted a befuddled gaze to Ethan as if he were the solution to this sticky problem.

"Mr. Johnson," Ethan began. "Jason Joe. I don't want to drag the authorities into this, but I will unless you stop insisting you're engaged to marry my wife."

The nurse stopped all pretense of working on Libby and looked from one man to the other.

"He's right." Libby jumped in with backup. "I'm not going to marry you, Jason. I never was going to marry you. And I *am* already married to Ethan, whether you believe it or not."

Jason Joe looked, for a second, as if he might cry, but then the Johnson family trait of mulish obstinance made his chin jut forward in denial. "I'm no fool, Libby Ann. You show me your marriage license and I'll kiss you on the cheek and wish you well.''

Marriage license. Libby's gaze turned helplessly to Ethan, who simply lifted his shoulders in a ''there's-always-a-catch'' shrug. ''Okay, then,'' Libby said, giving in to the inevitable. ''We will. We'll show you our marriage license.''

THE FRENZY OF activity that followed blurred into one continuous rush to the altar. The trip to Texas was postponed a few days, and avoiding Jason Joe while taking care of the technicalities of getting married in New York City consumed Libby's every waking hour. Ethan insisted their civil ceremony be as *civilized* as possible and sent Libby and Sallie shopping for new clothes, while he and Alex made arrangements for a small reception afterward at his office. Everywhere Libby turned, she seemed to run into Jason Joe and his insistence that she stop this *nonsense* and return home with him—no questions asked.

She thought about it. She really did…in the few moments she had to think between an exhausting day and a dream-filled night. It was the dreams that stopped her. The dreams of Ethan realizing he loved her beyond reason and wanted her beyond all things. The dreams of being in his arms and in his heart, of sharing a marriage that was more than just a contract. Then, suddenly, the moment had arrived and Libby said, "I do," with a lump of anxiety in her throat, a fledgling hope in her heart, and Ethan's promise that everything would work out right.

ETHAN PACED FROM his bedroom where Libby slept to the sitting room window to the door of the kids' room, then retraced the steps in reverse. He stood beside the bed and watched Libby sleep, then rubbed his jaw and paced some more. It was done. A deal, signed and sealed. The bad idea was now a legal contract. A marriage.

He rubbed his jaw some more, stopped to stare out the window again, smoothed the covers over a sleeping Alex, brushed a strand of silky hair off Sallie's china white cheek, then walked back to the sitting room window and stood, rubbing his jaw. He didn't know what craziness had possessed him the last few days, but he'd certainly let it run its course. He'd claimed to be Libby's fiancé, then her husband, then he'd married her to give truth to his impulsive lie. All along, he'd told himself it was for Libby, to protect her from an overzealous boyfriend, and an overprotective family.

But that was a lie, too. He'd done it to hold

her, to keep her in Sallie's and Alex's life, to stop her from leaving them as Diane and Neesa had done. He'd done it out of desperation, in the hope that this time he could keep the little-girl joy shining in Sallie's eyes, keep her talking in complete sentences, keep her laughing. He'd done it to stop Alex from drifting any further into himself and the make-believe of video games, the only world an eight-year-old had any control over. He'd done it to keep his kids in touch with a world that continually let them down and stole away people they loved.

Turning, he walked in to check on Libby. The cast on her arm was neon pink, and her fingers looked swollen where they emerged from the plaster. Her other hand was tucked beneath her cheek and her hair dusted the pillow in spiky silver-gold strips. She sighed softly, and he thought she was the most beautiful sleeper he'd ever seen. Next to Sallie. And Alex.

Married. Ethan let the word sit in his mind. *Married.* He mouthed it. *"Married,"* he whispered aloud.

It had been a bad idea from the start, Ethan knew that. It was wrong and deceitful and dishonest. But, in his heart of hearts, he didn't regret taking the action he'd taken. And he wasn't a bit sorry he'd seized the opportunity when it presented itself. And, in the quiet of early morning, while his little world slept in peace, he knew that it would all work out right.

LIBBY'S ARM ITCHED, her stomach churned, and her head ached. The probable cause of the itch was the cast. The source of her anxiety was most likely the imminent reunion with her family. The headache could be a result of the tension of the past few days combined with the pressurized air inside the airplane. But Libby was inclined to lay the giant's share of the blame for all her maladies on the man who was sitting across the aisle. Ethan Redwine, her husband. *Husband*. Yikes.

The plane hit a pocket of turbulence and Libby cradled her broken arm against her, as if that was going to help.

"Okay, Libby?" Sallie asked, her little legs thrumming the seat cushion excitedly. "Doeth your arm hurt?"

"A little," Libby answered.

Ethan looked at Libby with concern...and a tinge of wariness. She'd been pretty quiet ever since the civil ceremony yesterday afternoon. The reception had been pleasant, the whole affair planned to make her as comfortable as possible.

But she'd kept looking over her shoulder, expecting Jason Joe to show up and declare her marriage null and void in the eyes of Texas. He hadn't made an appearance then, or since, and she alternated between believing he'd finally given up and gone home and wondering what he might be telling her family. She'd called her mother to tell her, but between giving a not-entirely-correct report on how she'd come to break her wrist and when, exactly, she'd be home, the news of the wedding never quite came out. Libby knew it was cowardly, but told herself that face-to-face beat a person-to-person phone call. Especially, since she never knew which person—or how many—she'd be talking to. Besides it gave her a little extra time to get used to saying the words, "Hi, Mom, Dad. I'm married."

Married. Yikes.

"Hey, Libby, I found the secret key!" Alex leaned around Ethan, holding out the video game as if she could see his score on the tiny screen. "I did it!"

"That's great, Alex," she said, with a smile that faded as the boy settled back and the plane began a final descent. She had fifteen, twenty minutes—maybe less—to compose a lucid explanation for the family. They'd want to know how she'd broken her wrist, if she'd had a good flight, and who she'd brought home with her. They were expecting her to arrive with Jason Joe. They were expecting her to marry him. They weren't expecting any surprises.

Of course, there was always the possibility that Jason Joe had arrived home ahead of her, spilled his guts, and garnered support for his theory that her marriage was a sham. The very thought of all the mischief he could make made her stomach churn, all the more.

"You look a little green. Do you need another pain pill?" Ethan asked, leaning across the aisle. His touch on her sleeve was a light, reassuring contact, a warm awareness she wished she could pretend she didn't notice. "I can ask the attendant to bring you a glass of water."

"Ask her to bring me a fake ID and a dark wig. The only thing that's going to make me feel better is to get a new identity before this plane touches down."

Ethan cleared his throat. "I, uh, believe you already have...Mrs. Redwine."

Libby gulped, her gaze flying to his, her heart leaping into her throat, her thoughts clearing like clarified butter. "On second thought, give me that whole bottle of pills. Maybe I can be comatose before this plane reaches the terminal gate.''

"It isn't going to be that bad, Libby. You'll see. This is going to work out just fine. There'll be no pressure to marry Jason Joe, no wedding plans to circumvent, no explanations to make. Trust me. Our plan will work perfectly.''

She frowned, unable to remember what their *plan* was. "If you think my family won't ask for an explanation...''

"You don't have to give them one.''

"You don't know my family.''

"Then tell them we met at the Trevi Fountain, fell madly in love and got married the minute we landed in New York City.''

"But that's not the truth.''

"This week, it is,'' he said confidently.

"What about next week?''

"Let's take this a step at a time, okay? And the next step is to get through this week with your family.'' He held out his hand, palm up, and Libby took the pain pill he offered. "Take this,'' he said. "You'll feel better in a few minutes.''

"Daddy, look.'' Sallie turned from the window. "I thee Tektheth. Look, Libby! Look.'' She pointed at the clouds rushing past. "Tektheth!''

Libby swallowed the pill dry, figuring a little

discomfort was good for her. After all, she was about to face her family and lie like Pinocchio. Except, it wasn't entirely a lie. She had gone to Italy to marry the man of her dreams and she was returning with a husband...even if he wasn't the one she'd thought she would be bringing home. If she let her imagination run free, she could do a good job of convincing herself she'd fallen madly in love with Ethan. So that part wasn't a complete falsehood. The Leonardo da Vinci airport wasn't the Trevi Fountain, but they *were* both in Rome. She had gotten married in New York City...even though the ceremony hadn't happened the *minute* they'd arrived. She and Ethan were, in fact, married. For real, if not for always.

Make it mine. The words came back to her suddenly. The wish her heart had made at the Trevi Fountain. Without her permission, of course. Foolishly, without a doubt. She'd wished to meet a man as passionate and romantic as Dominic Carlucci—only not as hairy—fall madly in love and get married before her plane landed in Austin. And here, beside her, was Ethan, her husband.

Okay, so he wasn't romantic. And she hadn't seen him bare-chested, so she didn't know about the hairy part. They weren't madly in love. Madly in lust was more like it. Libby still couldn't look at him...even with the aches in her wrist and stomach and head...without remembering his kisses and wishing he would kiss her now, here. But they were married, about to meet her family, and lust really had no place in this fairy tale.

Libby stroked Sallie's bobbing head. The Waldron family didn't know what was in store for them, she thought. Not only an unexpected and unknown son-in-law, but grandchildren, too. Sort of like the grow-a-date gag gift her brother had given her a couple of years ago. You dropped a capsule in water and, instantly—or pretty quickly, anyway—a sponge grew into your "date." Only this time, it was a ready-made family. Alex, Sallie and Ethan—her own personal wish dropped into the Trevi Fountain and grown into a family. Maybe, from now on, she'd be a little more careful what she wished for.

"Look, Libby!" Sallie bounced in the seat and pointed some more. "Tektheth!"

Libby looked out the window as the Austin airport came into view. *Tektheth!* she thought. Yikes.

THE CROWD AT THE AIRPORT didn't seem overly large or particularly rowdy. Ethan scanned the faces, looking for a pair of eyes like Libby's. Or maybe a look-alike cuteness around the nose. But, other than a whole family of redheads, no one stood out in the group waiting to welcome the arriving travelers. Ethan herded Sallie and Alex through the door and into the airport, while balancing three carry-on bags and running block for Libby. He didn't want her getting jostled by the exiting passengers, who were in a hurry to meet family, friends or business associates in the terminal.

Libby certainly wasn't hurrying. She'd kept dropping behind, as if there were no one waiting for her, and he'd had to keep dropping back to stay with her. But he'd said nothing to move her along, letting her set her own pace, face down her own dread. He'd simply walked beside her and prevented the kids from rushing too far ahead. But the ramp wasn't that long, and after taking a deep and audible breath, Libby followed him into the open.

Ethan wished he could take her good hand and hold it, but he was weighted down with the luggage and the kids, who when faced with a sea of strange, smiling faces, stopped dead in their tracks. They weren't moving, and Ethan was caught between their solid little bodies and Libby, who seemed to be hiding behind him. "Okay, let's get this show on the road," he said, taking matters into his own hands and stepping aside so that he no longer blocked Libby from view.

"There she is!" The call came from one of the redheads, and suddenly the waiting area sported several cardboard signs all of which bore some variation of the message Welcome Home! Congratulations, Libby and Jason Joe! One long banner unscrolled, read It's About Time You Said Yes!

Ethan took it all in in a glance and realized that this boisterous group had turned out to welcome home the Prodigal Daughter and the hometown hero who'd rescued her from the perils of the big city. Ethan wondered if he should just yell *"Surprise! She married me,"* as an icebreaker.

"Libby!" A woman, a redhead, lunged forward and grabbed Libby in a hearty hug.

"Hello, Mom." Libby smiled and gave a one-armed hug in return.

Mom stepped back, then hugged Libby again. "Oh, I'm so happy you're home. We were so worried about you being in that dangerous, awful city all alone. I was never so relieved when Jason—" Libby's cast apparently made a sudden impression. "Why, sweetheart...whatever happened to your hand?"

"Thweetheart broke it," Sallie informed the

woman seriously, as if only another woman could possibly understand. ''Libby fell and broke her writht.''

''And now she can't play Donkey Kong Land with me.'' Alex stepped forward, putting himself protectively close to Libby. ''Except she did play one game left-handed.''

''Welcome back, Libby Ann.'' A tall, bulky man, whose copper red hair was mixed with silver-gray, put his arm around her and hugged her close against his side.

''Hi, Dad,'' she answered, hugging him back as best she could. Another redhead, a younger, bulkier version of Dad, approached, and soon there were three brothers standing around, waiting their turn to welcome Libby home. There were other women, too, although not redheads, and they all seemed to belong with one or the other of the Waldron men, and were just as eager to greet Libby and be a part of the group hug. There were children, too, of various awkward ages. All boys, all but a couple, redheads like the rest of the family.

There were covert glances at Ethan, too, and the children. Dark-haired, dark-eyed Alex and Sallie, who didn't exactly blend into this group. One of the boys grinned as he caught sight of the

Game Boy riding low in Alex's jacket pocket. "Hey, did Aunt Libby show you how to get the secret key?"

Alex's expression changed from watchful to interested, and he nodded enthusiastically as his hand went to his pocket and whipped out the video game faster than Wyatt Earp ever pulled a gun.

Then someone raised his voice above the general chatter and asked, "Hey, Libby. Where're you hidin' Jason Joe? He swore he wasn't comin' home without ya."

"Yes." Someone else picked up the question. "What've you done with him, Libby?"

Ethan heard her gulp, but then she flashed him a smile that made his heart stop. With a touch of her hand, she drew him and the kids forward for introductions. "Mom, Dad, this is Ethan, Alex and Sallie Redwine," she said, as if just saying their names made her happy. "Ethan and I are..." She giggled softly, as if what she was about to say was so strange and wonderful, she could hardly contain it. "We're *married*." With her free hand, she feathered the wispy, silky bangs on Sallie's upturned forehead. "And these are *our* children." Ethan heard her swallow hard a second time before her voice offered up a wobbly "Surprise."

Sallie's smile beamed at the assembled, shocked faces above her. "Thurprithe!" she said brightly. "I *like* Tektheth!"

THE DOOR CLOSED, shutting Ethan and Libby into a bedroom so frilly pink and feminine a man could go blind just looking at it. Which, now that he'd spent a couple of hours with Libby's family, he figured was the underlying reason for the color scheme. If, of course, any male had ever been allowed across the threshold at all. Until now. Until she came home with *him,* the *husband.*

"You can take the top two drawers." Libby pointed to the pale pink dresser. "And I'll move some of the stuff out of the closet, so you'll have room to hang up a few things."

"I didn't bring a lot of clothes," he said. "Are you feeling okay? You look a little pale."

"You don't look so healthy yourself." Sinking onto the edge of the mattress, she flopped backward, resting her casted arm across her middle and letting the other hand dangle off the bed. "I thought they behaved pretty well, considering that you came as quite a shock to them."

"Hmm." Ethan followed his gaze to the bed,

and after a moment's contemplation, he lay down next to Libby. "How many times would I have gotten slapped on the back if they *hadn't* been so shocked?"

She laughed, a soft, silky, wonderful sound. "I don't know. But I thought you held up well."

"To the back-slapping? Or the oft-repeated sentiment that I must be a hell of a man to have stolen you out from under the ever-alert nose of Jason Joe Johnson?"

She turned her head toward him, and he decided she looked very pretty against a background of pink. "I'm sorry I couldn't get across the room fast enough to save you from the arm-wrestling match with Grampa George. He's challenged every date who's ever walked through the front door. For a while, I tried being ready and waiting to run out to the car, but Grampa just followed me outside and accused my date of being too chicken to arm-wrestle him. It's a wonder I ever got asked out a second time."

"I'll keep asking you out, no matter how many times Grampa nails me."

Libby raised her eyebrows. "Did he beat you?"

Ethan smiled. "Oh, yeah."

"Fair and square?"

"Are you kidding? He's got that table rigged at practically a forty-five degree angle. Haven't you ever noticed how uneven it is?"

"You know, I guess I've never looked at it that closely. No wonder he always wins." Her laughter made the mattress shake slightly beneath him and Ethan rolled onto his side, propping his head on his fist, so he could watch her. "He did come up to me after your match and say that he guessed he could get used to having an *I*-talian around...if I was sure I meant to keep you."

Ethan grinned, knowing he meant to keep her...regardless of her intentions toward him. "One of your cousins...Clipper, maybe?"

"Kipper," she corrected him.

"Did you know he speaks Italian?"

"He does?"

"Well, he asked me to dance."

Her giggle was delightfully soft and sweet. "What did you answer?"

"I was on my best behavior, you know. First time meeting your family and all. I said yes, of course." Ethan grinned down at her, wanting to kiss her more than he'd wanted anything else all day. "So, Kipper brought me a beer and stood by while I downed it."

She frowned up at him. "Are you drunk?"

"Drunk from looking at you, Libby Ann."

Her nose scrunched in distaste. "Please don't call me that. It's bad enough being in my old rose-colored bedroom with you. I don't need anything else to make me feel like a little girl."

"I guess I could call you *Ducky.*"

She groaned. "Who told you?"

"Grampa George was eager to tell me all kinds of things about his only granddaughter. Aunt Azalea added the information that when you were born your hair looked like the fuzz on a newly hatched duckling."

Libby eyed him suspiciously. "That's all they said?"

"Yes. Oh, except for your Uncle Lake...or was it Shake? He mentioned that you waddle when you run and your voice gets this kind of *quack*-y sound when you have a cold."

Her hand went to her nape and absently fluffed at the hair there. "And that's it?"

He nodded, barely containing a grin. "Oh, I almost forgot. One of your cousins did say something about the way your hair makes that little ducktail in back."

Her hand dropped like a rock and she rolled her eyes. "Okay, so now that you've wormed the nickname out of my relatives, I have to warn you that calling me 'Ducky,' or any variation thereof, could cause serious problems."

"For me or you?"

Her chin came up. "Just forget you ever heard that ridiculous nickname and we'll get along fine."

"I hope so, because this isn't a very big bed."

Her blush arrived, charming in pink, and she drew her left arm across her eyes. "What am I doing, Ethan? I should have just told them the truth the minute we stepped off the plane this afternoon."

He let her regret drift halfway to the ceiling before he said, "You did. You told them we were married, and that, Libby, *is* the truth." Pocketing the kiss for a better time, he pushed upright. "I'm going to check on Sallie and Alex, make sure they're not driving your folks crazy. I'll tell them you took a pain pill and are going to rest for a while."

She nodded, not removing the arm that still covered her eyes. "I should have you send Mom up and get it over with. She's dying to talk to me alone, you know."

He leaned down and pressed his fingertip to her chin. "Jason Joe Johnson isn't the only man in the world who ever played quarterback, Libby.

Trust me. I'm not going to say anything to anyone that isn't, well…mostly true. Now, stay here and rest, and maybe when I come back upstairs, I'll find you *in the pink*.'' He waggled his eyebrows in case she looked. She didn't.

''Very funny,'' she said solemnly. ''Just don't come back *singing the blues*.''

''Don't worry. I don't want to mix up any *purple prose* tonight. That would be just too *ducky*.''

She tossed a pillow at him, but he caught it and tossed it back before taking a last, blinding look around the frilly room and leaving to go in search of his children.

''LOOK, DADDY! I'm making friendth with Paw and Makth.'' Sallie was sitting on the glassed-in porch with the ugliest dog Ethan had ever seen sprawled across her lap and a small gray schnauzer watching from a stubby-tail length away.

''She's very gentle with the dogs,'' Mary Ann, Libby's mother, said.

Ethan crouched beside his daughter and offered the back of his hand to Paw to sniff. ''You love the dogs, don't you.''

Sallie nodded vigorously and stroked Paw from his motley head to his puglike curl of a tail. ''Ith Libby athleep?''

"She's resting." He met Mary Ann's inquiring look with a reassuring smile. "I think she'll be in the pink tomorrow, though. This isn't the first time she's broken something, is it, Mrs. Waldron?"

There was a flash of surprise in the eyes as blue as Libby's. "I guess she told you she broke that same wrist her senior year at Beauregarde High?"

Ethan nodded. Actually, she'd told the doctor, but Ethan had been in the room and heard the story of the earlier break, so that counted. "Cheerleading practice," he said, as if he knew the details well. "One of the girls in the pyramid formation sneezed and Libby fell. I think that was a worse break than this one, though. The doctor said he thought she'd be out of the cast in five or six weeks. Possibly even sooner."

"I hope so. I still wish she'd let Dr. Brannigan take a look at it. He's taken care of her since she was a baby." Mary Ann bit her lower lip. "I guess I may as well mention this, because someone's bound to slip and say something about it. We…the family…were planning a big wedding for Libby and Jason Joe, once they got back from… Well, of course, that's neither here nor there now. But, well, I was wondering what sort of marriage ceremony you and Libby had?"

Ethan rubbed one of Paw's incredibly soft ears. "A civil ceremony," he said. "We were in something of a hurry at the time. It was a…sudden decision."

"Oh, I don't want you to think I'm unhappy about your marriage," she said hurriedly. "I mean, if it was love at first sight like Libby said, well, I can understand why you wouldn't want to wait to be together." She smiled at Sallie, who was now stroking Paw with one hand and Max with the other. Panda, it seemed, was out for the evening. "I know with young ones around the house, there's not much opportunity for a proper courting. And even if I do think it was a little, um, impetuous for Libby to jump off and marry you on such short acquaintance, well, that's really none of my…" Mrs. Waldron stopped herself and looked Ethan square in the eyes. "What I want to know, Mr. Redwine…"

"Ethan," he corrected her, with a sincere smile, feeling suddenly that he wanted Libby's mother to like him, that it mattered to him that she should.

"Ethan," she said, still watchful of him, still wary, but willing to accept him into her affections once she was convinced he would take good care of her daughter. "Libby's the only girl in the family, you know...and well, I've been imagining and planning her wedding day for years. It's a grave disappointment to me that I wasn't there when my daughter was married and that the ceremony didn't take place in a church.''

"It was a perfectly nice ceremony." He felt he ought to offer some reassurance, even though *perfectly nice* didn't really describe their rather austere wedding. Ethan knew Libby deserved better. He felt a twinge of regret at what he'd denied her.

"A big, elaborate wedding wasn't anything Libby seemed to want, but now that I know I can't give her one, well, it's just about to break my heart." Mary Ann paused, frowned, composed herself. "So here's what I want to know from you, Ethan. Would it be all right...would you *mind*...if we went ahead with the wedding we were planning for her and Jason Joe? Oh, I don't mean he'd be in it, of course. You'd be the groom, but it would be a nice ceremony, at the First Methodist Church, with all her family and friends looking on. You could even invite your people, if you wanted. Although, I guess it's a long way to travel from Italy."

Ethan started to correct her, but as he had no one to invite in Italy or anyplace else, he just shook his head. "It is a long way," he said.

"Well, they'd be welcome...if it's not too short

notice. This would mean so much to me, Ethan, I can't begin to tell you. It would mean a lot to Libby, too, even if she says it wouldn't. A marriage involves the whole family, you know, and we all want to be able to give her...and you, a real wedding, one you'll always remember. Even though you are already married, even though we really thought she was going to marry someone else. But going ahead with the plans for this wedding would mean a lot to the family...to me...if you wouldn't mind.''

"I think Libby's the person you should be asking, Mrs. Waldron," he suggested. "That would be her decision, not mine."

"Oh, she'll love it," Libby's mother assured him, the worried look in her blue eyes replaced with shiny new plans. "Especially if you'll sort of let her know that you'd like to do it. Could you do that, Ethan? Her aunts and I almost have everything planned already. You wouldn't have to do anything but be waiting for her when she walks down the aisle. Well, and say 'I do,' of course. Again. And this time, Sallie and Alex could be a part of the ceremony. Would you like to be the flower girl, Sallie?"

"Flower girl?" Sallie repeated. "Could Paw be the flower dog?"

Mary Ann nodded, apparently swept away with

the possibilities. "Alex can be the ring bearer, along with my grandson, Samuel, who's about the same size. We'll just have two ring bearers. Oh, this will be great. Wait until I tell Azalea and Tina the good news." She pushed to her feet, earning an irritable growl from Max and a leery glance from Ethan. "You will talk to Libby about this tonight, won't you, Ethan? There's so much that needs to be done." She stood there, wringing her hands while she planned, then suddenly she bent down and hugged Ethan around the neck. "Thank you for doing this," she said. "It'll be a wedding day none of us will ever forget!"

Ethan watched her bustle off, talking, planning to herself, and he wondered how she'd been able to con him so neatly. He felt a little as if he'd been hit by a Mack truck. A wedding. He'd just tacitly committed himself and Libby to a church wedding, under the eyes of Beauregarde, and to top it off, he was ninety-eight percent positive that Libby wasn't going to be happy about it. Hell, all the plans had already been made. He'd never even had a chance.

"Daddy?"

He looked expectantly at his daughter. "What is it, Sallie?"

"Can we go thee the llama now?"

"Maybe tomorrow."

Sallie seemed satisfied with that...or maybe she was just content to be holding a lapful of dog. Ethan watched her hands as she stroked the dogs in an off-beat, irregular rhythm that Paw and Max didn't seem to mind in the least. No matter what happened, no matter how many weddings he ended up having, this trip had already done wonders for the kids. Sallie had plenty to look forward to, and Alex was outside playing a boisterous game with a handful of the Waldron grandsons. Ethan could hear his voice occasionally calling out in answer to the other boys.

Okay, so Libby wasn't going to agree to go through another marriage ceremony with him. The only reason she'd agreed to the first one was that he was a damn good negotiator and she'd been in a rather pliable mood from the pain and the painkillers. He'd taken advantage of the opportunity. He'd admit it. But this time, the bargaining was bound to present more of a challenge.

On the plus side, he had nearly a whole week to persuade her...and pink was a very romantic color.

Chapter Nine

"No," Libby said without hesitation. "No."

"Your mother seemed pretty set on the idea. Maybe…?"

"No," she repeated. "My mother had bouquets and bridal veils on her mind ten minutes after I was born. My brothers all had lovely weddings, but she didn't get to *plan* those. She has no restraint when it comes to this sort of thing." Libby swept her hand to encompass the room. "I mean, look at all this *pink*."

Ethan looked and manfully kept his hand from rising to shield his eyes.

"With my aunts to help her, there'll be too much of everything. Too many flowers. Too much music. Too many people. Too much *pink*."

"We'll tell her no wedding," he said, tabling the subject until Libby was in a more receptive frame of mind. "Now, are you feeling all right? Does your wrist hurt? Did you find the bottle of pain pills?"

She stared at him across the pink bedspread. "Yes, no, and no, I didn't because I'm not in pain. You don't have to take care of me, Ethan. I'm perfectly capable of taking a pill when I need one without being reminded."

Ethan regarded her from the other side of the bed, wondering why she was so agitated all of a sudden. She'd handled everything so well. Maybe she just didn't want to admit that her wrist was bothering her, or maybe she really did want to have the big wedding but didn't like the idea of not being able to have any say in it. Or maybe... His gaze dropped to the pink lace pillows on the pink satin bed and then lifted, quickly, inquiringly to hers. Ah, he thought. And then he had to take a couple of deep breaths because of the thoughts he was thinking.

"You're right," he said, casually pulling back the puffy satin comforter to find—what else?— pink sheets underneath. "I won't pester you about the pills again. Is it all right if I occasionally ask you how you're feeling? Or should I just wait until you tell me?"

"I'll tell you." She looked from the head of

the bed, which he was uncovering, to the foot of the bed, which he wasn't, before she trained those wide blue eyes on him again. "What are you doing?"

He did his level best to look innocently surprised. "I was thinking I'd go to bed. I didn't get much sleep last night and this is the only bed I've been offered, so I figured this is where I'm supposed to sleep."

"Oh," Libby said, and blushed. "Oh. Right. I hadn't…hadn't thought about where you'd sleep."

"No reason you should have." Which, of course, they both knew was a lie. There was only one bed in this room and they were about to share it. A double bed. Not big enough to allow them to avoid each other. Not enough room to ignore a heady sexual attraction. Not enough space to dilute the awareness that was already weaving a subtle tension through the air. Ethan began to unbutton his shirt. He didn't have any idea where this might go, but one way or another, he was going to bed.

"I should say good-night to Sallie and Alex," she said suddenly, and started for the door.

"They're already asleep. I tucked them in over an hour ago, played a couple of checker games

with Grampa George—he cheats at that, too—
talked to your dad about the history of Beauregarde—very interesting town you grew up in,
Libby—and by the time we all said good-night
and I stopped in to check on the kids, they were
fast asleep.''

''Oh,'' she said. ''Oh. I guess everybody wondered where I was all evening, huh?''

''They assumed you'd taken the pain pills and
were sleeping. I had to distract your mom a couple of times from coming up to check on you.
Figured if you wanted company, you'd come
downstairs.''

''Thanks,'' she said, but didn't sound much
like she meant it. ''I did nap off and on. And
unpacked.'' She put her hand on the doorknob.
''Maybe I'll go in and say good-night to Mom.''

He nodded. ''Why don't you do that? When
she shows you the plans for the waterfall garland
she wants to drape across the front of the church,
you can tell her you have no intention of going
through another wedding ceremony.''

Libby sank onto the edge of a plush, prissy,
very pink boudoir chair and sighed. ''I guess we
ought to talk about...'' Her voice trailed off when
she looked up and saw that he was peeling off his
shirt. She blinked, then closed her eyes and swal-

lowed hard. "You don't have too much hair on your chest," she said.

Ethan looked down, feeling a bit defensive, wondering if he ought to offer to shave off what he had or run out to the drugstore and stock up on Rogaine. "It's a matter of genetics," he said, wishing he'd kept his shirt on. "Hairy chests don't run in our family. At least, that's what I've been told. My father died when I was still a boy and my mother wasn't particularly...hairy. Not that I ever noticed, anyway."

Libby smiled faintly. "I'm sure you would have noticed. Is your mother...?"

"She died a little over a year ago. When Diane left, Mother moved to New York to help me with the kids, and then she died very suddenly a few months later. Went to sleep one night and didn't wake up. A heart attack." He steadied himself against the tightness that pulled at his chest and throat. "It was a tough time."

"I'm sorry, Ethan."

"It was really rough on the kids. I worry a lot about them. They've experienced too much loss to be so young."

"I'm not sure age makes it any better. I'd say your loss was more catastrophic than theirs. At least they've always had you."

He didn't see it that way, but he didn't want to discuss it, either. "Sallie has already attached herself to your dogs," he said. "I had to forcibly remove Paw from her bed. She was trying to hide him under the covers."

Libby's laugh was soft and soothing. "I can't believe she got him upstairs without Mom or Dad catching her. The kitchen is as close as I could ever get to sneaking them into the house."

"Sallie's very resourceful when she wants to be." He sat on the edge of the bed and took off first one shoe, then the other, feeling a physical tightness join the building emotional tension inside him. How was he ever going to sleep in this room, in this bed, and not touch her, kiss her, make love to her? He should have been too dog-tired to even notice how lost she looked amid all this pinkness. He should have been too sleepy to see the covert glances she cast at him and his not-completely-hairless chest. He should have known better than to marry her...even with the best intentions. With a sigh, he stood up. "I'll sleep somewhere else, Libby," he offered reluctantly. "I know this is uncomfortable for you."

Uncomfortable? Libby blinked and took another look at the bedroom she hadn't been able to move out of soon enough. She would never be comfortable in this room, no matter who else was, or wasn't, in it. "Once, when I was fifteen, I fixed this room the way I wanted it. Painted the ceiling black and the walls this icky gold color, glued glitter around the windowsills and light switches, and hung these horrible sun, moon and star mobiles across the windows. It looked perfectly awful and I loved it. Really loved it."

"But your mom and dad hated it."

She nodded, smiling at how wonderfully rebellious she'd felt in her gaudy black-and-glitter-gold bedroom. "They were convinced I'd joined some weird cult. Or worse, that I'd dropped out of the National Honor Society. Mom stood it as long as she could...about a month...but she just *knew* I couldn't be happy in such depressing surroundings, so while I was away at cheerleading camp, they redecorated for me. Somewhere Mom had read that a nice blend of pinks is *uplifting* to the adolescent psyche. I couldn't convince her otherwise, and the room's had this blushing demeanor ever since."

"So did this *rosy* perspective have a beneficial effect on you?"

She rolled her eyes. "I guess that would depend on who you asked."

"I'm asking you, Libby."

"I think I'd have been happier if I could have kept the room the way I liked it. But there was only so much rebellion in me, and it didn't seem worth upsetting everyone over. Then my dad got sick and the color of my room became pretty unimportant to all of us." She picked up a pink-striped pillow and hugged it against her chest, watching Ethan and thinking he was a definite addition to the room as a whole and to her life, in particular. "You know, I think you're probably the first man I've ever entertained in this sinfully pink boudoir. My mother is probably not going to get a wink of sleep tonight, just thinking about it."

"Thinking about it could keep us all awake." Ethan walked around the corner of the bed and stood looking at her. Shirtless, shoeless and so sexy Libby wished she had a Polaroid of him so she could blow it up, hang it on the wall and give this room a reason to blush. "I need to know where you want me to sleep, Libby. Here—" he gestured at the bed "—or downstairs on the living room couch."

"Downstairs?" She repeated, seeing disaster written all over that idea. "Oh, brother. All I need is for Mom to find you on the couch. She'd be on the phone telling the entire town that our marriage is on the rocks and the wedding is back on. Jason Joe, the hometown favorite, would regain the Chief Groom title, be repositioned at the altar of the First Methodist Church, and you, my friend, would be on the first plane out of here...probably with a butt full of buckshot.'' She shook her head, set the pillow aside and thought there must still be some black-and-gold rebellion left in her soul. Because she'd just had the most shocking idea. The most delightfully, obvious, shocking idea. ''You have no choice but to stay here, Ethan. You're the first man ever to be invited to stay in this bower of bliss and—'' she turned the latch and locked the door ''—I'm not about to let you escape.''

''I could go blind from all this *pink*.''

''Then you'll just have to keep your eyes closed.'' She switched off the overhead light, leaving the room lit by a small bedside lamp. ''Then, again, you might want to keep them open.''

His eyebrows went up. Just a little. Just enough. His gaze slid to the bed, back to her. ''That bed doesn't leave a lot of room for compromise.''

Libby thought back to the way he'd kissed her, the sweet swirl of desire she'd felt then, the anticipation she felt now…and smiled. "Then we'll have pancakes," she said.

"Pancakes? Now?"

She lifted her shoulder in a seductive shrug, eased her sweater sleeve over her cast, then tugged the hem up over her head and off. "Sometimes, Ethan, you just have to be spontaneous."

ETHAN'S KNEES WENT WEAK, but fortunately, Libby strolled over to where he was standing, her hips swaying with an innocent and deadly sensuality, her expression set on seduction. Which was okay with him. Okay, hell. He'd never wanted a woman so much in his life. Libby was a breath of fresh air, unexpected, beautiful, vibrant, impulsive. Five minutes ago, he wouldn't have given odds of a million to one that anything like this could happen, and suddenly she'd made up her mind to exorcize the room's pink demons and he couldn't have escaped if he'd wanted to. Which he didn't. Even if he suspected her impulsive seduction had more to do with latent rebellion than undiluted desire for him. Even if she had regrets in the morning.

Her arms went around his neck, the cast laid heavily against one shoulder as she drew his head down to hers, and Ethan gave up on the ethics of the situation. He knew only that her breath was sweet and warm and her lips were soft and warm and her body was warm and so sexy a man could lose weeks of his life in it. Which wasn't a bad idea, he thought as he picked her up and carried her to the bed. They'd spend six weeks in bed getting acquainted, and then, maybe, they'd talk about breakfast.

A HEADY BOLDNESS BLAZED through Libby as she sank into the mattress and pulled Ethan down with her. The conviction that she was finally exactly where she wanted to be gave her nearly as much pleasure as the feel of Ethan's lips on hers, his arms around her, the hardness of his body pressing into hers. She should have thought of this years ago, she decided. Except years ago Ethan wouldn't have been here to tempt her, tease her, fulfill her fantasies. No other man had ever filled her senses with this new and unfamiliar urgency. She wanted him. She wanted to be naked in this bedroom, in her bed, with him. She wanted to make love with him, and she wanted to wake up in the morning and find him still there beside her. She had wished Ethan into her life, and somehow she was going to wish him into staying in her life, wish him to be the partner she wanted, wish him into the husband she'd dreamed of having.

Because, unlike any other man she'd been with before, when Ethan kissed her, she felt strong. Capable. Cherished.

Ethan shed his pants and Libby wriggled out of hers. She unclasped her bra and tossed it, carelessly, across the pink lampshade and then felt a warm, rosy blush steal over her bare breasts. Ethan cupped the blush in his hands and heated it with tantalizing circles of his tongue. He lathed each willing peak in turn, then nibbled at the silken hollow between them even as his hand slid across her stomach and down to stroke her thigh. Libby wanted to cry out her pleasure in groaning repetitions of his name, but his mouth closed over hers, silencing her, giving her a new taste of delight, a new sensation to distract the voices inside her, a new urgency to occupy her thoughts.

He loved her with his hands, covering every inch of her with his exploring touch. And he loved her with his lips, trailing kisses over her skin until she was hot and wet and so needy she ached. She loved him with the five fingertips she had available, feeling the muscular hardness of his body, the wiry perfection of the hair that dusted his chest, the thick, hot desire of him that pulsed against her touch. She even managed to use her right thumb to stroke along his side and was rewarded with a rough command to stop *tickling*.

She stopped. But only because his stroking hand had found a sensitive spot low on her belly and she couldn't think, much less move. He rolled away from her once to locate a condom, but rolled back almost before she had time to miss his warmth. Then Ethan made love to her in earnest. No more teasing caresses, no more playful nips at her lips. He kissed her hard and long and deep, replacing lighter touches with a sweeping hunger that demanded possession. All or nothing. He asked her body to respond and promised fulfillment in return. He requested her complete participation and pledged passion as reward. He took her surrender and allowed her to command his. No part of her denied him access, and when his full weight pressed her down and down into the smooth pink sheets, Libby took him inside herself. Took his body into hers. Took his lips with her own. Took his passion and his need, and in a single splendid moment, when there was only the beating of one heart, the singular stroke of one consuming passion, she gave him all the colors of her love, knowing she could never take them back.

Sometime later, Libby sighed with deep satisfaction. "I will never be able to think about this room again without blushing all the way to my toes."

He kissed her shoulder, her breast, her lips, her nose. "Me, neither."

Laughing, she pressed the weight of her cast against his shoulder and pushed him over onto his back. "Oh, yeah?" she accused, rolling on top of him. "Prove it."

So he did.

As TIRED AS HE WAS, Ethan couldn't fall asleep. He lay in bed next to Libby, whose breathing was deep and even. She'd denied taking any more pain pills, but he felt sure she was still feeling the effects of the medication she had taken. And once again, he'd taken advantage of the situation. Of her.

Cupping the back of his head with his hands, he stared at the ceiling, trying to find some redeeming factor in the way he'd treated Libby. Now that he'd met her family, he could understand her fear that they'd steamroller her through a wedding she didn't want, with a man she didn't love. The Waldrons were nothing if not completely positive they knew what was best for their only daughter. But had Ethan really saved her? Was being married to him all that much better than being married to Jason Joe Johnson?

Oh, Ethan didn't doubt that he was a better choice for Libby. She deserved a bigger life than she could find here, and he wanted to give it to her, wanted to show her places she'd never seen, wanted to give her the independence she would never be able to gain in this small Texas town. He knew, without question, that he and Libby had much in common and shared the same basic family values. Putting together deals was his business and he was very good at it. He'd known before he'd entrusted his children's care to her that he and Libby had a great deal to offer each other. He knew their marriage, though outwardly impulsive and impractical, held the promise of a long and fulfilling relationship.

But the fact remained that the hastily contrived marriage hadn't been her choice, any more than the elaborately planned wedding would have been. She'd told him once that men always seemed to be standing in line to protect her, to keep her from getting her shoes wet in a rain puddle, to shelter her from sunburn, or fight the battles she was deemed too fragile to fight. He'd told her at the time, he thought women and men had to be responsible for their own happiness. Then he'd decided she was the mother his children needed and he'd run roughshod over her hopes and dreams and wishes to save her from disaster...and secure her for his own.

She said something, low and unintelligible, and he turned his head to watch her sleep. Dark lashes dusted her cheek, and her hair was as gold as a harvest moon in the soft darkness. He tried to imagine her with flecks of black paint in her hair and glitter all over her hands, tried to visualize her standing up to the determined, redheaded forces of her family. But he was either too tired or the pink room overpowered the image, because all he could see right now was Libby's fascinating and fragile beauty. And what he felt was a fierce wave of protectiveness, possessiveness, and... passion.

LIBBY AWAKENED AS DAWN penciled in the first lines of morning, and her first thought was how warm she felt and how deliciously good. Usually her bedroom greeted her with so much girlish glow that she had to keep her eyes closed for at least five minutes before she gathered enough courage to face her surroundings. Not this morning. Not after last night. Never again.

Stretching her legs, she ran her foot over Ethan's hair-rough calf and smiled. Then she smiled some more. Mmm, she thought. Mmm. Slowly, so as not to miss a single stirring sensation in her body, she let herself come to full wakefulness. Her arm itched a little beneath the cast, but the dull ache was gone and she could wiggle her fingers some, which meant the swelling had receded. The brain fog had vanished, and the only physical complaint she could come up with was a vague thirst. Libby didn't think she'd felt this good since...well, for a long time.

Beside her, wide, warm and male, Ethan sighed and slept on.

Okay, Libby thought. This was the deal. She was home. She was awake. She was married. Sharing-a-bed, sharing-a-name, sharing-sex married. Her memory of just how she'd come to this intriguing state of affairs wasn't completely clear, but she was willing to wait and see what developed. A wish, after all, was a wish.

"COCK-A-DOODIE-DOO!   Cock-a-doodie-doo!" Ethan awoke with a start to the sound of a rooster crowing. He pulled a pillow over his head to muffle the screech, but the rooster pulled it off and got closer to his ear. "Wake up, Daddy," Sallie said. "We gotta thee the llama!" Then she crowed again.

He peeped at her from under the pillow. "What time is it? Daybreak?"

"Time to go!" She began jumping up and down on the bed. "Grampa George thayth we better get going 'cauthe llamath wait for no man, but little girlth have to."

"Where's Alex?"

"With Tham."

"Sam?"

"Yeth. And Robbie and Jumper and Flip." Sallie jumped high and landed, legs flat, on Ethan's stomach. "They're all boyth, Daddy. 'Thept me. Now Grandma Mary hath another girl bethide Libby. Me!"

Grandma Mary? Ethan struggled awake, realizing Libby was no longer in bed beside him, and her absence made the whole room decidedly blue. "Where is Libby?" he asked his daughter.

"Downthtairth. Waitin' for you."

"Actually, she's right here," Libby said from the doorway. "Waitin' for you."

Ethan smiled, happier to see her than he would have thought possible. Dressed in faded jeans and a white T, she looked rested and relaxed, and he wanted nothing so much as to pull her under the

covers and kiss her everywhere. Then he'd probably want to kiss her *everywhere* again. "Tell me
one good reason I should get out of this bed and
you shouldn't get in it," he said.

"Llamath, Daddy." Sallie began tugging at the
sheet. "The llamath are waitin' for me."

Libby grinned at him. "And that," she said,
"is about the best reason you're going to find."

"Couldn't I get just one kiss good morning?"

Sallie sighed with impatience, leaned over and
bussed his cheek. "Now will you get up,
Daddy?" she asked. "Now, can we go thee the
llamath?"

Ethan looked wistfully at Libby, then he turned
Sallie toward the door and patted her encourag-
ingly on the back. "Now we can go," he said.
"Just as soon as I get dressed and have some
breakfast."

Sallie scampered to Libby's side and took her
hand happily. "Me and Libby'll be waitin'.
Hurry, Daddy. I don't want to mith nothin'!"

IF THEY MISSED ANYTHING, Ethan couldn't imagine what it might have been. From Cousin Juner's
llamas, to Uncle Hoot's livestock, Aunt Azalea's
garden and florist shop, Uncle Twig's lumberyard,
Uncle Knot's shoe store, Aunt Pip's craft sup-

plies, and the kittens in Cousin Tom's garage, Ethan saw Beauregarde from top to bottom. Along with Libby, Sallie, Alex, Sam and three other redheaded nephews whose names Ethan couldn't keep straight. He was introduced to so many cousins, uncles and aunts, it was hard to imagine that Libby wasn't kin to everyone in the state of Texas.

"I warned you it was a big family," she said at one point.

"You should have given me a study guide," he said in answer.

"Don't say anything like that to Aunt Tina. Genealogy is a sore subject with her."

"I can imagine, with this many branches on the family tree."

"No, she just doesn't want anyone to find out her real name is Methalia." Libby winked at him. "At least all the last names are Waldron."

"Except yours," he pointed out, feeling possessive and proud.

"Oh, yeah" was all she said.

"JASON JOE GOT BACK in town last night." The carhop at Bud's Burger Shack handed information and burgers through the window of the minivan. "I haven't seen him, but my friend Taffy's boyfriend said he was washing his Ram at the Spot Not around midnight.''

Libby smiled and took the burgers, not wanting to encourage any discussion of Jason Joe Johnson. ''Okay,'' she said. ''Who had the cheeseburgers and who ordered plain?''

Hands went up in the back and middle seats and boys' voices yelled out their preferences. Ethan took the burgers and passed them out accordingly, unwrapping Sallie's and folding the paper down around the bun before handing her the less-mess package.

The carhop left and came back with drinks and more information. ''I'm in the marching band,'' she said, with a snap of her chewing gum. ''I was on the curve of the question mark when we spelled out that question Jason Joe asked you. I wanted to be the dot at the bottom, but Greg Tuttle sits first chair drums and he got it.''

Libby nodded and wished they'd taken the kids to get ice cream instead. ''It was a very nice question mark'' was the only comment she could think of to make.

The carhop flipped her ponytail, took the twenty dollar bill Libby offered and made change from the coin changer at her waist. ''I heard you're getting married next Saturday down at the

First Methodist. Some Italian guy you went all the way to Rome to get. Has a funny name. Redeweeni or somethin' Italian-soundin' like that.''

"You shouldn't give credence to everything you hear in this town,'' Libby said.

"Huh?'' The carhop looked puzzled, but Libby was already backing the van from the drive-in space and hoping fervently that none of her nephews had picked up on that particular pronunciation of her new last name.

Ethan held two cardboard carriers containing all the drinks and watched her as she spun gravel pulling out of Bud's Burger Shack. She asked him if he had something to say simply by raising her eyebrows.

"Does Jason Joe usually wash his sheep at the car wash at midnight?'' He asked suspiciously.

"Sheep?'' she repeated with a frown. "Oh, you mean...'' She began to laugh. "Ram. He has a Dodge *Ram* pickup.''

From the middle seat came a snort, then from the back, a snicker, and then a general round of guffaws, which grew into some high humor.

Ethan looked at the boys and one small girl who were having some fun at his expense. Then, suddenly, he put his head back and laughed, too.

And that was the moment Libby knew for sure that she loved him.

Chapter Ten

"Look what I found." Mary Ann Waldron met Libby as she came through the front door. In her hand was a blue satin hanger and on the hanger was a white satin gown. "It's my wedding dress."

Libby knew immediately where this was headed, and she tried, valiantly, to look pleasantly surprised by her mother's good fortune. But this was manipulation, pure and simple, and she wished she could think of an excuse to go back out the way she'd come and avoid the question altogether. But Ethan, Sallie and Alex were right behind her, already crowding into the front hall to see.

"Oooh," Sallie said. "Thatth pretty."

"Pretty," Alex echoed, although without much enthusiasm. "Has anybody seen my Game Boy?"

"Well, it's 'bout time you got yourself back here." Grampa George spoke in gruff syllables from the corner of the room. "And showed me how to work this here video game."

Alex was around Libby like a shot, eager to retrieve his game from the clutches of a rank amateur.

"That's pretty," Ethan said, his voice going directly over Libby's head to bring a bigger smile to her mother's face. "It doesn't look as if it's ever been worn."

Mary Ann ran a loving gaze over the lace bodice. "It was worn once and it's been packed away ever since, waiting for the day Libby Ann would wear it at her wedding."

"I'm, uh, going upstairs to change," Libby began, hoping that a mention of the evening's activities would distract Mary Ann. "The barn dance starts at seven-thirty and—"

"Oh, there's plenty of time for you to try this on. I'm dying to see how it looks on you." Her mother was halfway up the stairs before Libby could blink, much less think of a legitimate protest. Other than that she didn't want a big wedding and that she really saw no point in trying on her mother's wedding gown when she'd already *had* a wedding. And the whole point of *that* wedding had been to keep this one from happening. "I've made a couple of alterations," Mary Ann continued as she made the first landing. "Just guessing, you know. Took in the waist a bit and did a couple of tiny little tucks across the shoulders, but I think it's going to fit you just fine now, and—" She paused to look down with a distracted air. "Aren't you coming up with me?"

"Mom," Libby said firmly, but with an apology in her voice, "I don't need a wedding dress."

Mary Ann's face fell with disappointment. "Well, of course, you don't have to wear it. I just thought...hoped...you'd be sentimental enough to... Well, never mind, then. You can buy something new, something not so girlish and..." Her voice trailed off, and the hem of the gown crimped against the stair step in dejection. "It was silly of me to think you'd want to wear this old thing, anyway."

"Mom..." Libby tried hard to keep any hint of her exasperation hidden, but she knew it came out sounding like a miserable plea for understanding. "It's not the dress. Your wedding dress is lovely, and I'm sure it would fit me just fine. But we've already discussed this. I've had one wedding and I don't want another one. Especially not a big church wedding, like the one you and the aunts have your hearts set on.''

"Oh, Libby," Mary Ann said sadly. "It's all planned. You don't have to do a single thing...except try on this dress so I can make sure it fits. And if you really don't like it, we'll go shopping tomorrow and get something else." She frowned. "But now that I think about it, your Aunt Belle had a beautiful wedding gown. It was layers and layers of pink tulle...I'm sure you've seen pictures of it." More of the white satin crumpled into a puddle on the stairs. "It would look just wonderful on you, Libby. If she still has it." Mary Ann laughed, her spirits rising again. "Of course, she has it. Every one of us got married with the thought that we'd one day have a daughter who'd wear our wedding gowns. And since you don't like mine..."

"I didn't say anything about not liking it," Libby protested.

"Well, then, come up here and try it on, please. Unless you really think you'd prefer Aunt Belle's pink tulle."

Libby looked to Ethan, hoping he would save her, but his gaze traveled from the white dress to the mother to the daughter. Then he shrugged. It was a weak excuse for one, but it was a shrug, nonetheless. "It can't hurt to try it on, Libby," he said.

She knew then and there that there would be a wedding on Saturday. She was going to walk down the aisle of the First Methodist Church in her mother's wedding dress. The same dress she was about to put on now, so that her mother could check the seams and pin the hem and make whatever other alterations were necessary. The only concession her family seemed willing to make was that Ethan would be the one waiting for her at the end of the aisle, instead of Jason Joe. Libby sighed, because just once, she would have liked to say no and have someone pay attention. "Okay," she said. "I'll try on the dress right now. Sallie? You want to help me?"

"Yeth," Sallie answered, eager to get her hands on the white satin.

"I'll help," Ethan volunteered, too.

"Oh, no, not you, Ethan." Mary Ann swept on up the stairway with the dress. "It's bad luck for you to see Libby in her wedding gown. You know that."

"I'll keep my eyes closed," he said, grinning. "I promise."

"Mom." Libby called out a gently insistent reminder. "Ethan and I are already married. Remember?"

"How could I remember when I wasn't there? Your own mother not invited to her only daughter's wedding." Mary Ann sniffed, loudly, at the offense. "Besides, you can't be too careful these days," she said, as if that put an end to that argument. "Now, up we go."

So, up all three of them went.

"WHAT HAPPENS AT THIS kind of thing?" Ethan asked. "Two barns get together and dance?"

"You have led a sheltered life, haven't you." Libby led the way inside a brightly lit, cavernous old structure. "At a barn dance," she explained, "there's one barn, which stays put, and a bunch of people, who don't. Can you dance?"

"Like a dream."

"Two-step?"

"No, 3-D. Sometimes in living color."

She stopped, her gaze meeting his with a tinge of shyness before she flashed him a smile that nearly stopped his heart from beating. "Well, this won't be anything like that."

"Like dancing in my sleep?"

"No, and you won't get any sleep here, either."

One step more and he realized that was the un-varnished truth. As he and Libby paused in the big open doorway, the music stopped and Uncle Billy, the town's leading pharmacist—Ethan remembered him from an earlier trip to the drug-store—grabbed the microphone, sending bone-jarring squawks reverberating through the rafters before he announced, "Here they are, finally! It's the happy couple, come to dance with us!"

There followed a general round of clapping, a couple of solid backslaps from some redheaded kinfolk who were close by, and a volley of good-natured good wishes. Before Ethan knew what was happening, he was pulled away from Libby and propelled through the crowd to the wood-crate stage. "Speech," someone yelled. "Give him the mike, Billy."

Ethan gulped, hoping they weren't serious, hoping the music would start and the barn would dance. Or the people could dance. He wasn't particular.

But Uncle Billy maintained his master of ceremonies role. "Let me introduce him first, Hector." He cleared his throat, importantly, and tapped the mike, which dutifully whined. "Now, there's nobody here who was more surprised than me when Libby turned down Jason Joe Johnson's proposal right in the middle of the football game and said she was going to Italy—'' he put the accent on the middle syllable, making it sound like It-*towel*-y ''—to marry a foreigner. And there isn't a single person in this town who thought she'd do it. But she did and we're all here tonight to celebrate with an old-fashioned barbecue and barn dance. You're all invited to a genuine Texas-style weddin', which is gonna happen Saturday at two o'clock at the First Methodist Church, and we'll party after that, too. But for now, let's give a big Beauregarde welcome to the man our Libby picked over all the others she coulda had. Ethan Red Wine.''

Billy managed to accent all syllables equally that time, and Ethan supposed he should be glad for small favors. Redweenie wouldn't be his choice for a family nickname. Across the sea of smiling faces, he sought Libby's, wanting her to come up on this crate and save him from disaster. But she stood in the center of the crowd, looking breathtaking and sassy in her all-white outfit, looking as if she was enjoying his moment in the spotlight and hadn't any intention of helping him out.

Ethan quickly composed a few words appropriate to the occasion…and promptly forgot them when Libby flashed him a megawatt smile. He knew suddenly that he was the luckiest man in heaven or earth to be sharing a frilly, pink bedroom with her. And when he opened his mouth, that's exactly what he said.

"CHEER UP," SHE TOLD HIM later, as they walked another lap around the deserted and dark corral. The music of the Hill Country Band filtered through the soft October night and swirled lazily toward the starry sky overhead. "I thought it was funny. I've been trying for years to change my image, and I think you may have done it in one little slip of the tongue."

"Your parents are never going to speak to me again."

"You won't be that lucky. Forget it, Ethan. It's not as if I've been sneaking you up a ladder and into my bedroom at night. We're married. For real, if not for always."

He stopped walking. "What does that mean?"

She frowned. "What?"

"That not-for-always business."

She stopped, too, and faced him, her eyes shadowed by the brim of the cowboy hat, her dimple flashing then fading in the moonlight. "I know you never had any idea of this becoming a *real* marriage. I know it's just a contract. I help you with Sallie and Alex, you help me save face in my hometown and, as a bonus, keep me from being hustled into a wedding with Jason Joe as the groom.''

Ethan thought it sounded like a bad idea, put like that. ''So now you're being hustled into a wedding with me as the groom.''

She shook her head. ''There is a difference, Ethan.''

''There is?''

''If I'd married Jason Joe, he'd never have let me go.''

Ethan hadn't ever considered the possibility that he'd have to let her go. That she'd expect him to honor the unspoken terms of their contract and release her from her duties when she asked him to. No, he hadn't expected that at all. If he'd thought about it, he probably would have assumed that down the road, once Alex and Sallie were grown, he and Libby would come to an amicable parting of the ways. Unless they'd become comfortable enough with their roles that they stayed together out of sheer convenience. Not exactly the happily-ever-after ending the Beauregarde community was celebrating with such gusto tonight.

''Hey, Daddy.'' Alex's voice, his vowels already blending into a softer, slower drawl from exposure to the Waldron cousins, came from the opposite side of the corral, where the light from inside the barn spilled across the gate. "What're you and Libby doin' out here in the dark?"

"Hey, Daddy." Sallie climbed onto the gate next to her brother. "Hi, Libby. Whatchu and Daddy doin'? Are you kithin'?"

Libby seemed unsure of what to say, so Ethan answered for her. "We're dancing," he said, drawing her into his arms, picking up the rhythm of the Tennessee Waltz. "We're dancing in the dark."

"Hmm." Sallie kicked her heels against the slatted wood gate. "Grampa George thaid he bet you were out here kithin'."

"Grampa George doesn't know everything." Ethan tightened his hold on Libby and kept dancing, telling himself he hadn't signed a contract he couldn't renegotiate, reminded himself that he didn't have any faith in romantic illusions...like realizing he was crazy sick in love with his wife.

LIBBY KNEW SHE SHOULDN'T be doing this.

No matter how many times her dad said she was the most beautiful bride in the history of the world.

No matter how many times her mother cried and said this was the happiest day of her entire life.

No matter how many times Ethan said it was just another ceremony, just an extension of the unwritten contract they'd already made.

It had been one thing to agree to marry him while her head was foggy with painkillers and she was frantic to escape what seemed an inevitable future with the man her family wanted her to have. It was another thing altogether to stand up in the First Methodist Church in front of the good people of Beauregarde, Texas, and make vows she knew she couldn't keep.

Gathering the satin skirt in her hands, Libby lifted the hem and paced from one end of Pastor Thompson's study to the other. Sallie, her only companion at the moment, sat in the pastor's chair, pushing and pulling herself up to and away from the desk with a repetitive squeak. Beneath a garland of blue flowers, Sallie's wispy hair sprouted around her face in straight black sprigs. *She has hair just like yours,* Mary Ann had pronounced earlier, after a dozen unsuccessful attempts to curl Sallie's hair.

Libby smiled sadly. She and Sallie had a lot in common. Mainly, their love for Alex and Ethan, who were in some other cubbyhole of the church, waiting for the appointed hour to become a family in the eyes of God and Beauregarde. She started pacing again. She shouldn't do this. Not to Alex and Sallie. Not to Ethan or herself. It was a bad idea. A wrong idea. Dishonest. And the very thing that made it dishonest was that Libby wanted so much for this wedding to be real, wanted desperately for these children and their father to be her family, wanted more than anything for the wish she'd made at the Trevi Fountain to come true. She wanted Ethan to love her. Not for a while. For forever and always.

But now that she was ten minutes away from marrying Ethan again in a no-excuses ceremony, Libby had to face facts. And the fact was, she was in love with Ethan Redwine and that's why she couldn't marry him now. That first ceremony had been as much her doing as his, no matter how she'd like to pretend otherwise. She might not have been clear-headed at the time, but her heart had clearly known her secret desire...and seized the opportunity to get it.

But how could she bring everything to a screeching halt? Should she send Ethan a note? Ask him to drop into Pastor Thompson's study to do some serious renegotiations? Figure out some way to tell her husband that she couldn't marry him, again, because she had been foolish enough to fall in love with him?

Sallie slipped from the chair and disappeared under the desk, popped into sight again, then vanished anew. The door to the study opened and Libby took a deep breath. She had to decide. She had to stop this romantic nonsense that Ethan was going to take one look at her in her mother's wedding gown and forget the terms of their contract. She had no choice but to close her eyes, grit her teeth and admit "I can't go through with this."

The words hung there for a second before Libby opened her eyes and saw that it wasn't her father or Pastor Thompson who'd come in.

"Well, hot damn," Jason Joe Johnson said. "I knew all the time it was me you really loved."

Then he picked her up, like an oversize satin pigskin and headed out the door to his Ram.

"TELL ME AGAIN, SALLIE." Ethan tried to be gentle as he squeezed Sallie's trembling shoulders. "Tell me what she said."

Sallie hiccoughed away a fresh set of tears. "Libby thaid, 'I can't go through with thith.'"

Sitting behind Pastor Thompson's desk, Mary

Ann sobbed into a handkerchief. "Go on," Ethan requested softly.

Sallie sniffed and raised her chin. "And then he thaid, 'I knew it wath me you really loved.' And then they left."

Ethan's jaw ached. His stomach churned. Every muscle in his body was tense. "Did they thay— *say*—where they were going?"

Sallie shook her head. Alex touched his arm. "Dad? Maybe Sam and Robbie would know. They know all the roads around here."

Ethan looked at his son's worried face, his daughter's misery, and knew that, for their sakes, he should let Libby go. Let her leave them now instead of later when it would be ever so much harder. And he couldn't even blame Libby for running away. If he hadn't pushed her so hard, manipulated her into this situation, tried to save them all with one desperate gamble...

He clenched his fist at the irony. He'd thought Alex and Sallie needed a mother, and suddenly Libby had dropped into their lives like a wish he'd made without ever a hope it could come true. She was perfect, the exact woman he would have chosen if he'd gone out searching, and he'd believed it was worth any sacrifice to get her to stay with them, love and care for them. What he hadn't figured out until just now was that it hadn't been Alex and Sallie who needed Libby.

It was he.

Cold, no-nonsense, skeptical Ethan, who needed the warmth and wonder that was Libby. She'd even told him as much. *Alex and Sallie have you,* she'd said. But he hadn't seen the truth, hadn't seen that his kids were all right despite the adult dramas surrounding them, that they would be all right as long as they had one constant, steadying anchor. Him.

But who would anchor him if he let Libby go? He needed her. He wanted her. He…loved her.

Putting Sallie away from him, he straightened abruptly and headed for the study door. "I'm going after her," he said.

"Go, Daddy, go!" Sallie ran up and hugged his knees for encouragement. "Kith her."

He touched her cheek and took one of her tears for luck. "I'll do my best, Sallie."

"What about the wedding?" Mary Ann asked, blowing her nose.

Ethan jerked open the door. "We'll ask Libby, once I bring her back. If she says no, then the wedding's off. And no one—not even her mother—is going to say another word to her about it." He strode out the door, purposeful and proud of himself for finally standing up for Libby's rights.

He just hoped he could maintain that same supportive attitude if she told him she'd decided to marry that lughead who kept trying to carry her off.

ETHAN BORROWED Uncle Hoot's old pickup and, not knowing which way to go, randomly chose to turn right and head out of town toward the interstate. About four miles from the church, off to the side of the two-lane road, he spotted a solitary figure in a long white dress walking toward him. Oh, my God, he thought. She'd finally had enough of Jason Joe's caveman tactics and killed him with her bare cast.

But as he pulled up beside Libby, she looked composed and calm. Her cast looked okay, too, although there might have been a couple of dirty smudges on the neon pink wrap. "Hello, Ethan," she said, with no audible notes of distress, sounding as unconcerned as if she were passing him on Fifth Avenue and just being routinely friendly. "How are you?"

He drove on, made a fast U-turn and came up next to her again, this time going in the same direction. "I'm fine," he answered. "And you?"

"I'm good, thanks. Really good. Now."

"Now?"

She bobbed her head agreeably, her lips forming a pleasant Mona Lisa kind of smile. "Now that I've decided I'm never getting married."

"Again." He leaned out the side of the old truck, keeping one hand on the steering wheel, keeping one hand free in case...well, just in case. "You're never getting married *again.*"

She narrowed her blue eyes on him. "I consider our first marriage an invalid contract."

His heart sank, then came back to fight. "I'm not going to let you go that easily, Libby. I...can't." She kept walking, and he kept creeping along at two miles an hour beside her. "Look, can I give you a ride somewhere?"

"No. I prefer to walk from now on."

This was not going well, he thought, then shored his courage to try again. "Okay, but it's going to take us a long time to get back to New York."

She waved a hand in airy dismissal. "I'll tell you what I just told Jason Joe Johnson. I'm a free woman, and I'm thinking of traveling around the world. Maybe even as far as Istanbul...once I find a job." She sighed with the practicality of it all, then her chin came up with a new determination. "And if I want to walk that far, I will."

"Okay. I'll walk with you."

"And what about your children?"

"*Our* children can walk, too," he said. "At least, I hope you think of them as ours because..."

She stopped walking and he stopped driving and they looked at each other as a car came tearing up the road toward them and passed at a speed of considerably more than two miles an hour. "That's Ricky Taber and Brian Schwartz," she told him. "They're on Jason Joe's football team."

Ethan considered that information without much concern. "Wonder where they're going in such a hurry?"

The Mona Lisa smile returned. "Maybe someone they know ran off the road and into a muddy creek bed. Maybe someone's Ram is stuck up to its rear bumper in mud. Maybe someone they know got pushed into the mud, himself, by a woman who was tired of being carried around like a dumb old football."

Ethan's gaze dropped to the hem of her gown. "How could someone escape without getting stuck themselves?"

Libby lifted her skirt to reveal shoes, and ankles, encased in thick red mud. She gave a little shrug as her blue eyes met his. "Won't Mom be happy I saved her dress?"

"So happy, she won't care that you don't want the wedding she always dreamed you'd have."

"She'll never be that happy." Libby started walking again.

Ethan let up on the brake and the truck rolled forward. "Believe me, she's a changed woman. When you get back to the—" He stopped, corrected himself. "*If* you go back to the church, she's going to ask you if you want to go on with the wedding, and when you say no, she won't ever mention a wedding to you again."

Libby shook her head. "Why not?"

"Because I'm your husband and I told her not to."

"And that worked?"

"I don't know. Wanna go back and find out if standing up to her works?"

"I was sort of thinking I'd just quietly leave town and…"

"You have to go back, Libby, one way or the other."

Her chin came up. "Did you come out here to rescue me? Because if you think I'm—"

"I came out to see if you needed some help

getting away from that crazed kidnapper. It's not a rescue attempt at all. More like a reinforcement." He gathered all the courage he could muster. "Actually, it's more like this...I came out to ask you not to marry him without giving me a chance to change your mind. I came out here to tell you I've broken the terms of our contract and there's a few things we need to renegotiate."

"*You* broke the contract? How did you do that?"

Ethan braked, turned off the ignition and got out of the truck, leaving it sitting not quite off the road, not quite in it. He fell into step with Libby. "I fell in love with you," he said simply. "Me. The one who made all the noise about romantic nonsense and never falling for that moonlight illusion again. I fell for you like a..." He shrugged. "Name your analogy. Like a ton of bricks. Like a leaf from a tree. Like a—"

"Knot on a log," she suggested. But she was smiling. *Thank you, God! She was smiling!*

"Like a man who had enough sense to finally realize he'd met the woman he'd always wished to find."

Libby walked a few more paces, her muddy shoes making a squishy sound on the dry pavement. "I wished for you, Ethan," she said, the teasing note gone from her voice. "I made a wish at the Trevi Fountain and suddenly, there you were. Oh, not at the fountain, of course. But that's where it started." She stopped the squish, stopped the talking and looked at him for a very long moment. "Are you just saying you love me because you want someone to take care of Sallie and Alex, because you can hire a nanny if that's all—"

"If it's important to you, we will hire one. So that I can spend time convincing you how very important you are to me. Me, Libby. Not just my kids. Me." He pressed his finger to her lips, tracing their slight tremor. "I love you, Libby. For real. For always. And it has nothing to do with Sallie and Alex. They have me. I'm their anchor. You're mine."

She blinked back a tear. "We'll both be their anchor, and we won't need a nanny. Oh, Ethan, I really wanted to marry you today. Pink garland, sappy wedding songs, my mother's dress and all. It was part of my wish, too, like Sallie and Alex. A sort of bonus wish. I always thought the wedding was what my mother wanted, but now I think it's what I'd like more than anything else."

He kissed her then, long and hard and hungrily, there on the road leading out of Beauregarde and toward the interstate. She kissed him back, her cast weighing against his shoulder, keeping him from flat out drifting away with sheer happiness.

When she pulled back, there was a new light of confidence in her eyes and in the sexy gaze she draped over him. "Before we go back, there's something I have to do. Something I'd like even more than that brouhaha of a wedding we're going to have later this afternoon." She undid his bow tie with a tug and pushed him back toward Uncle Hoot's old pickup. "Something you're going to like better than a wedding, too. I promise."

"Libby..." He tried to sound shocked, cautious, all the things a husband probably ought to sound like when his wife was intent on seducing him in an old truck beside a Beauregarde thoroughfare in the middle of the afternoon. "Think about this. You're wearing your mother's dress."

She opened the door and shoved him down onto the seat before she hiked her skirts and followed him in. "She should never have painted my room pink."

And at that particular moment, Ethan was thrilled to pieces that she had.

Epilogue

Dear Gina and Jessica,

My wish came true! There, I had to get it down on paper before I burst with the news. I met the perfect man, fell madly in love with him, and we got married— *Yes! Married!* All before I stepped foot in Texas again. Can you believe it? Oh, I know, it sounds like I just made this wish up as things happened, but I swear it's really, truly, honestly what I wished for when I threw my coin into the Trevi Fountain that day.

I know what you're thinking, Gina, and no, I haven't been guzzling the cabernet and I'm not drunk. Unless you want me to admit I'm drunk on love, which is sappy but the

God's truth. I haven't even gone near a bottle of wine since I became a mother.

Yep, you read that right, too. I have two beautiful children, Alex, eight, and Sallie, four, who are so bright and funny and beautiful.... Oops, I mentioned that twice, didn't I? Only because it's true, though. They're really wonderful and I'm just crazy about them. I know that, technically, kids weren't part of my original wish, but I've always wanted children, so I think that has to be counted as a sort of *unspoken* wish, don't you?

Come to think of it, you guys probably don't have a clue what my wish was, do you? Okay, maybe a *clue,* but you know what I mean. There wasn't much time to talk after we each tossed in our coins and made our wishes. I guess we were supposed to keep it a secret, anyway, but I probably would have told mine, if I'd had the opportunity. Anyway, I'll just tell you so you'll know how incredible it is that my wish came true. I'm still amazed. Especially since my *official* wish was just that I'd some day return to throw another coin into the fountain. But in my heart of hearts, I wished I'd meet a tall, handsome, romantic and passionate stranger who'd fall madly in love with me and marry me before I had to step off the plane in Austin and face my family. I know that sounds really cowardly, but you guys don't know my family.

I never dreamed it would be my wish that came true, but who do you think I met at the airport in Rome, while I was trying to get a flight home? You'll never guess, so I'll tell you. Ethan! Ethan Redwine. And he's my husband. Yes. For real. And always, too. We met at the airport when he yelled at me for taking his little girl to the bathroom. Well, he didn't actually yell at me. He was just scared when he couldn't find Sallie. But then he asked me to help him take care of her and Alex on the trip home and then we spent some time in New York City and then my ex-boyfriend showed up and tried to kidnap me, but I broke my wrist and Ethan had to marry me then. It was sort of the principle of the thing, you know. Then we came here to Beauregarde and fell in love for real and got married again at the First Methodist Church. I wore my mother's wedding dress and Sallie was our flower girl and Alex was the ring bearer, and it was so perfect, I'm sitting here sighing and smiling as I write it down.

Uh-oh. Sallie just came in to ask me when she's going to have a baby sister. She has a lisp, which is improving with therapy, so she says it in this cute way…baby *thithter*. And I don't know what to tell her, because Ethan's standing behind her looking at me with this *look* and…

I'll write more later. Please write soon and let me know how you are, and if, maybe, the wishes you wished in Rome came true, too. Let's keep in touch!

Love and hugs,
Libby

Take 2 bestselling love stories FREE

Plus get a FREE surprise gift!

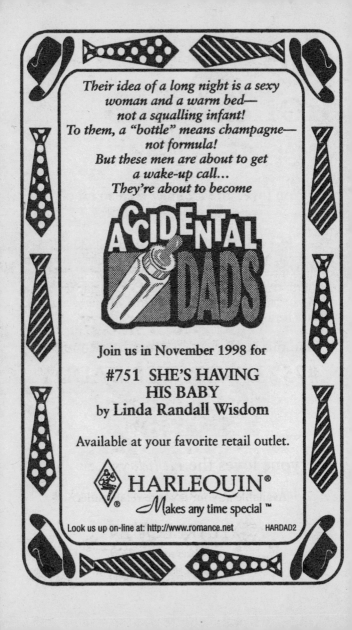

**SEXY, POWERFUL MEN NEED
EXTRAORDINARY WOMEN WHEN THEY'RE**

Destined for Love

Take a walk on the wild side this October
when three bestselling authors weave wondrous stories
about heroines who use their extraspecial abilities to
achieve the magic and wonder of love!

HATFIELD AND McCOY
by HEATHER GRAHAM POZZESSERE

LIGHTNING STRIKES
by KATHLEEN KORBEL

MYSTERY LOVER
by ANNETTE BROADRICK

Available October 1998
wherever Harlequin and Silhouette books are sold.

HARLEQUIN®
Makes any time special ™

Silhouette®

COMING NEXT MONTH

#749 IF WISHES WERE...DADDIES by Jo Leigh
Three Coins in a Fountain
Jessica Needham wished to be left alone, particularly by Nick Carlucci—but she was having his baby. She'd convinced herself he'd never need to know—right up until she opened her door to find Nick on the other side....

#750 SIGN ME, SPEECHLESS IN SEATTLE by Emily Dalton
As the title star of the popular column "Ask Aunt Tilly," Mathilda McKinney dispensed advice to the lovelorn and the troubled. But who would advise Mathilda, now that drop-dead-gorgeous duke Julian Rothwell was steamed at her counsel—and demanded Tilly herself as payment!

#751 SHE'S HAVING HIS BABY by Linda Randall Wisdom
Accidental Dads
Caitlin O'Hara and Jake Roberts. They went together like peanut butter and jelly. Friends since the first day of kindergarten, they shared everything, including Friday-night pizza and war stories from the romance trenches. But there were some things you didn't even ask your best friend—like "Can you make me pregnant?" Or did you?

#752 DOORSTEP DADDY by Linda Cajio
The Holiday Heart
Richard Holiday: Single, sexy—and up to his ears in dirty diapers and raging hormones, toddlers, teenagers and kids in between! But was he ready to give up his bachelorhood? The three happy children made his house feel like a real home.... The only thing missing was a wife....

AVAILABLE THIS MONTH:

Look us up on-line at: http://www.romance.net